The Watchmaker's Wife

JANIS MACKAY

To Jeremy

BIG
BARK
BOOKS

First published by Big Bark Books in 2019

ISBN: 978-1-9161726-0-9

The paper used in this book is recyclable. It is made from low chlorine pulps produced in a low energy, low emission manner from renewable forests.

Printed and bound by Bell & Bain Ltd, Glasgow

Typeset in 11 point Adobe Garamond by Main Point Books, Edinburgh

Janis Mackay is an author, storyteller and creative writing tutor. The author of nine books for children, her first novel, *Magnus Fin and the Ocean Quest*, won the Kelpies Prize in 2009 and in 2013 *The Accidental Time Traveller* won the Scottish Children's Book Award. Janis lives in Edinburgh where she is currently doing a PhD researching mythology and its influences on self-reflective creative writing. To find out more visit www.janismackay.com

With love and gratitude I dedicate this book to my mother

Mary Mackay

and to my grandmother

Johanna

1

I'm in father's arms, swinging round and round.

Mother's at the window laughing then we're birling faster and faster and she's not laughing anymore. She screams, pulls at me. The room tips sideways then there's a crack. Glass smashes, splinters of it whirl round, like us, and catch the light as they fall.

I've a white thread on my forehead from that waltz. It's my first memory, dancing, singing, a waterfall of sparkling light – and being held. Even falling to the ground father pressed his strong arms tight around me.

It was that I thought of on the stone step of the church, not ten minutes wed, as father, shabby in his thin suit, shook loose a packet of confetti over me. I laughed, fighting to hold back tears then placed my trembling hand under the crook of my husband's elbow. I watched them go, my own father and mother, awkward alongside the better dressed Lockharts, walking too fast. 'Not even a piece of sponge-cake, mother?' My voice sounded thin, wavering. I picked a paper horse-shoe from my hair. 'There's a spread set out. Clara…Willie's sister… she's done a…'

Mother shook her head. Maybe my voice lacked conviction. Or I was scared father would fall down drunk, shaming me. Off they scurried to catch the horse-drawn cart that would bump and shoogle them back to Leith. I felt relieved and guilty for it. But I was a Lockhart now. Married to a watch maker. And at twenty five years of age an old maid no more. We were to live in the pretty town of Haddington. I was a somebody! And a somebody's wife. Haddington, Willie had told me, has a right pretty meandering river with swans. And a quaint old church, trees and a view of the hills. With respectable folk. Oh, it's nothing like your poor Leith, Willie said.

Two hours later, walking from my new sister-in-law, Clara's house, (where she'd put on a fine spread though few stayed for it), along the wide Haddington High Street, to the house I was to call home, I still couldn't shake the memory off me. Father, drunk and dancing all these years back with me in his arms and now here I was, married.

Married!

Willie slipped his arm round my waist and pulled me to him. 'There's nothing tae you,' he said. I shook my head, blushing. More of father's confetti fell from my hair, as if I was snowing. Willie did a wee hop and skip then. A few folk on the street cheered. Willie saluted them and clicked his heels together. I clamped my hand over my mouth, stifling a laugh, and my jittering teeth. Suddenly he scooped his arms under my bottom and lifted me up into the air. The small crowd laughed while I hit weakly at his shoulders, urging him to put me down, my dashing soldier. 'Wheesht now wee woman,' he said, jiggling me. 'You're light as a feather. And your husband is strong as an ox.'

'Husband,' I gasped, flinging my arms around his neck and clinging on for dear life. 'Husband'. The word frightened me. He wasn't tall but he *was* strong. I felt the hardness of his muscles against my chest. 'Aye, husband,' he said, and spun me round on the street. Haddington blurred. The onlookers were a dark clump, laughing, arms waving, then a horse and cart flew by, then a bay window, a snatch of white sky. I screamed. I felt sick and as nervous as a babe in arms. 'Dinny fret my bonnie dearie,' he said, slowing down and rocking me as though that's exactly what I was. 'Willie here will look after ye. Willie here won the War. Now, you and me, Johanna…' He swayed. I thought he was going to drop me but he righted himself and brought his face up close to mine. 'You… and… me….' I smelt the drink on him, saw red thread-veins on his nose. 'You... and… me...'

I closed my eyes. Willie crooned the words – *aye, you and me… oh you and me….*But in his song it wasn't Willie Lockhart and me. The face of James Melville, like a tender ghost, came to me. Of all days on my wedding day, I could see him, hear the ring of his voice. I want to marry a good woman, he said. *Aye, you... u...uuuu and me...* Willie's song cut back in on my memories. I smothered James Melville, image and echo. I snapped my eyes open and there in front of me was my husband, singing in the street for all the fine folk to hear: *'You and me Johanna, we're married!'*

I vowed then and there, being birled around the High Street in Haddington, that never again would I dwell on my dead soldier. I stifled a scream. It came out in gasps. I was all in a whirl. I, Johanna Blackie, was married. What was I saying? Blackie! I was Mrs Lockhart now! And here we were, in the peaceful respectable town of Haddington, on the threshold of our own house. He fumbled with the door handle, nudging me up his shoulder like a parcel. The door handle stuck so he kicked the door. It swung open with a creak and we were over the threshold; out of the light and into the gloom. He paraded me around the tiny dim place then lowered me to my feet. I tried to push away the sinking feeling. He'd made it sound like a palace. 'Welcome home, Mrs Lockhart,' he said, with a flourish of his wrist. But he knew it was small. His voice tried to swell the cramped hovel of the tiny house. I could hear that, but didn't want to look ungrateful. 'Aye,' I said, 'very nice,' and out of habit I curtsied.

'You're not a servant now,' he said, squaring up his shoulders. He seemed to fill the place. I flustered. What a fool. And there I was, my eyes landing on grime and dust, thinking how a duster would shift the first layer of dirt, then a wrung out damp cloth for the floor, with plenty ammonia. I felt disappointment plunge through me. He lied to me. That's what I thought. The so called palace was tiny, and no taps for running water that I could see, but I nodded, fixing a smile on my married face as the damp walls closed in. 'Anyway Johanna, I brought yer kist.' He pointed to my wooden chest on the floor. Perhaps he saw how I glanced about at the poky place for he said, 'aye, it's no much, but better than where you came from.' He stepped towards me wearing a look on his face that alarmed me. 'Way better than Leith.' His colour peaked. His eyes fell to my bosom. This was it, the duty. He was so close I could smell the whiff of whisky. 'And your husband's no common gardener like your poor faither. Oh no. Willie Lockhart here's a watch-maker.' He smacked his chest and cleared his throat. 'Wi' the auld tunes pulsing in his blood.' Then he winked at me, slapped his thigh, a one, two, three and four, then burst into, '*Step we gaily...on we go...*' He swayed as he sang. Was he dancing? Was he drunk? I tapped my toe along with his song. I was surprised when he pulled an old fiddle down from off a shelf. I didn't know he could play. He winked at me. He played along to his singing. '*Heel for heel and toe for toe.*' In that dim lit wee room he even managed a pas de basque. '*Arm in arm and row on row.*' I clapped at his capers. With his fiddle lifted high he twirled like a Highland Dancer then stopped, thrust his fiddle under his chin and winked at me. '*All for Johanna's wedding.*' Then he launched into the next verse.

Maybe it was the tune that took me. Maybe the cramped wee house. Or the fact of being wed. Whatever set it off I couldn't hold down this kist of memories. In a heart-beat the years folded back.

Father could fairly sing.

> *Come along, come along, let us foot it out the gether,*
> *Come along, come along, be it fair or stormy weather...*

Because it's a long trudge from the foot of Leith Walk up to Liberton. There – and back. Four miles at least and the morning's journey all uphill and in the winter dark both ways. From Leith everywhere is uphill. Thomas Blackie, market gardener, does the walk six days out of seven, forty-eight miles in a week. If you are born in 1860 and not of the gentry you think nothing of it or maybe curse it but thole it anyway with a bottle of stout and a bit company. And maybe you jump on the back of the milk cart for the steep hill up Liberton Brae, putting by some raspberries for the cart-man on the way back if it's the season.

Father smells of soil and cabbages, neeps, apples and well-rotted manure. His nails are aye rimmed with dirt but the long road and the outdoor work surely brings him some peace. Our tenement in Gordon Street is like them all: overcrowded, damp, a rabble of bairns and mother aye cleaning.

Leith. A dark conglomeration of high tipping tenements and chimneys. All of them creaking and blackened from the smoke of coal fires. Not like his green Liberton where good things grow, a paradise by comparison. He takes me, just the once. Mother is ill. Father hoists me up onto his back and I get a collie buckie up the Walk and he sings the whole way,

Gin a body meet a body, comin frae the toon.

He's in a fine mood. I sit in a golden field out in the sun and sift through the punnets and throw away the white strawberries. I am meant tae chuck oot the white yins and what do I do? Eat the whole damn lot!

The gold sun is on the grass and the men in the fruit bushes sing as they work. Edinburgh only reaches as far as Dalkeith Road. Liberton is countryside with wee cottages and fields, haystacks and scores of horses. The Liberton accents drawl slower. Father says the men at work have an awfy job understanding his fast way of talking. There's dockside twang in the Leith speech, and a course crust.

* * *

Willie's song ended. He put his fiddle back on the shelf. I clapped my hands together, swatting father, strawberries and the years back. My knees, under my blue dress, trembled. Blue. Not green. Bad luck for a bride to marry in green, mother had warned me. I smoothed down my dress. Willie laughed. I swung round to look at the window. What if the folk out on the street had their noses pressed up against the glass? Willie was panting. I thought it was the effort of the wee bit song and dance.

'The bed's through here,' he said, cocking his head towards the room by the kitchen. He took another step towards me then grasped my clammy hand. Mother had told me, I would need to do my duty. He clamped his fingers about my hand, clammy, urgent. The image of another hand tugged at me. But that hand was cold in the earth. And I'd long for him no more. I was married now. A married woman. My husband pulled me through to the other room. It was barely bigger than the bed. The air in the bedroom reeked of smoke and damp. 'Close the curtain,' was all I could say. Willie laughed and said I needna worry. The good folk of Haddington had seen it all before. I might find myself crying out, he said. My cheeks burned with shame. Then he was standing behind me, running his hand up and down my back. He was fumbling with the fasteners. I didn't want him to tear the dress. I felt a finger stroke the back of my neck. I was shaking all over. Then his hand was cupping my breast. He squeezed tight and I whimpered. 'Wheesht,' he mumbled, his breath coming thick now. 'Oh, you've fine paps on ye. Oh aye. Oh.' Tighter he squeezed. I bit my lip. 'A woman should be prood o thur paps.'

Father doesn't trust the tap.

Says he's seen what Cholera can do to a man so has a good excuse to drink beer. Father was aye thirsty.

A peen to see the puppet show
A peen to see him cry
A peen to see the auld man
Sitting in the sky...

We're whirling round and round. The shadows from two candles whirl too.

* * *

Willie hoisted up my skirt. 'Forget the fasheners,' he said, his words slurring. He pushed me onto the bed. 'Yer husband's a watchmaker. Guid wi his hands.'

* * *

We whirl, round and round. Father drunk as a Lord.

There's that hot sour smell from his breath and him shouting how he'll make his youngest bairn intae a highland dancer so he will.

***

The pillow smelt damp. Then it was wet. I was crying. My dress rode up to my armpits, all crumpled and Willie on top of me was grunting, pushing up and down. I thought the bed would break. I thought I would break.

***

Gin a body, meet a body, coming through the rye…

We're spinning round and round. Father staggers, hits his elbow off the table edge and a glass leaps and shatters on the floor. Mother screams. Father's cursing, and I fall onto the stone floor. Splinters from the broken glass cover me like confetti.

***

Willie stroked my damp hair, pushing it out of my eyes. 'Ye hurt yerself,' he said, tracing the white line on my forehead. His stubby finger pressed into my forehead. A guttering candle turns him into a ghost. The way it shuddered he was there then gone. 'Silly wee lassie,' he said. 'You should be…' He slumped back, leaving his sentence hovering. His head was next to mine on the pillow. Should be what, I wanted to ask, but he was snoring, asleep by my side.

Should be married to James Melville. The answer rose in my throat. Though I tried to swallow it deep but it came clamouring. I got up, took off my wedding dress and laid it over the one chair. Cold moonlight spilled over my kist. I opened it, then with shaking hands brought out my nightgown. Ye've made yer bed, I chided myself as I stepped into my fresh laundered gown. Then I l blew out the candle and lay down, crying myself to sleep.

2

I was born in 1895, same year as electricity though it's candles and gas I remember; the shadows on the wall and the pictures they make – of ghosties, goblins and old men with long beards. They're drunk too, swaying and shaking and when the wind echoes down the chimney they moan, we're coming tae get ye – Johanna!

Our house in Gordon Street in Leith is always full of folk; granny, aunties, neighbours, sisters, all bumping into each other, getting in the road, getting told to get out the way and everybody working. Sometimes one of the women's voices screeches like a knife over a tin plate. Sometimes they all whisper, their heads falling in to a dark circle. There's a lot of banging, stirring and thumping. The brown metal kettle pipes along with them, whistling and spluttering.

There's mother in her old faded pinny. There's that brown tea pot, and the trivet it stands on, the leather strap for sharpening razors that father has hanging by the door. What a strong salty smell coming from mother's stew. What a reek off father's old clay pipe.

***

I came to on that hard bed that first morning of my married life, thinking it was my own father supping his morning tea I was hearing. Then the dreams fled. That wasn't father. That was my husband. I panicked and hurried out of bed, fumbling in the dark for a pin to lift up my hair. I smoothed down my night-gown. By the sound of it my husband was in the kitchen taking his tea. Shouldn't I be the one to make him tea? I pushed aside the bedroom door and there he was, lit by a stub of candle and schlurping tea from a tin cup. He waved me away, saying he liked the first cup of tea to himself. I was to give him peace. So in the cool dark I went back to bed, feeling an ache at my hips, and a shame. I heard him lift the latch. I heard the snap-snap of his shoes on the pavement. Then he was gone. It wasn't yet dawn. I was used to rising early, but sleep tugged at me. 'Sleep's for the wicked.' It was mother's voice I heard. 'Yer married now lassie. Up and get to work.' So I did. Then I saw the blood stain on the sheet.

After the fine kitchen I was used to working in, the place in Haddington seemed a hovel. The town was nice right enough but our room and kitchen was hardly one of Haddington's finest. After being in service I'd got used to running water, now here I was, thrown back into the dark ages. To fetch water I had to go out to the back green with my bucket – like a woman at a well. In the kitchen there was not a plate that wasn't chipped or cracked and the damp patches were like pictures on the wall. The air was stale and the first thing I did was open the windows then I tied my pinny behind my back and put all my servant years into practice. I steeped the bed sheet in a bucket of salted water. A tear splatted into the feathering blood. Then it was good to be busy. I scrubbed, scraped, brushed, scoured and threw out the broken plates that were beyond repair. I had brought a box of dusters and such like with me. I was right in guessing that William Lockhart had nothing of the sort. I polished the wooden table with a mixture of beeswax, soap, white wax and turpentine and brought it up to a grand shine. I cleaned the windows with vinegar and newspaper. What a difference. I mended the torn curtains, boiled the pillow cases and black leaded the fire grate. By the time daylight faded the wee house smelled clean and fresh, and everything, not that there was much, gleamed. By five o'clock I had my pinny off and a hare stewing. I splashed water on my face and brushed my hair. I left it loose, for like Willie said, I wasn't a servant now.

I stood at the open door, enjoying the fresh air. Willie was right about the air in Haddington being cleaner. I don't know how long I stood there, fanning cool air across my face. A long time I waited for him, my thoughts spinning off. Being wed had made me dreamy. I thought it was because of the way he had pressed so hard into me. I felt split open. I thought it was that that forced open the gates I had shut tight behind me. For there I was; Mrs Lockhart, twenty five years old and not one day married, waiting in the scrubbed and dim place for my new husband to come home and memories bursting open like floodgates. I was back, a child again.

The day I leave Gordon Street the sun is shining.

Leith Walk is a golden river, and everybody on it has a spring in their step and a smile on their face. I'm fourteen, with hair as black as a raven's wing. Of course I've been up since first light and because it's summer that's early enough. Everything I touch I imagine it's for the last time. Even the damp cludgy out in the back green that early in the morning has its charm; the way grass grows up under your feet and the quiet of the cramped smelly place that Jemima and I spent thousands of fearful minutes in. Even the cold black stand pipe glistens. Splashing water on my face I listen to its scoosh and gurgle.

I run up the dipping stone steps, my face still wet and tingling. I know the shape of every step, and the smooth feel of the wooden banister under the palm of my hand. Tiny simple things are wondrous. I clutch at the smooth wood of the banister. This place is a part of me. Am I mad to be going away?

I lean against the door of the house and cry, then wipe my tears and push open the door of the house, plastering a smile across my face for mother at her cleaning, father at his porridge and Jemima wringing her hands and sobbing. I gaze for the hundredth time at my kist and make sure everything's packed neat. Not that there's much; two blouses, one change of vest, bloomers and stockings, one change of shoes, my bone comb, a blue ribbon, wooden bowl and a woollen shawl. And there are long cloths for binding my breasts for my chest is swelling and mother says they must be bound tight. Paps, she calls them and I blush.

Father has paid little heed to me these last few days. Now in the early morning of this, my last day at home, he bends over his porridge, spooning the thick gruel into his mouth.

'So – that's me then,' I say, my black coat slung over my arm and my kist at my feet.

'Aye, it'll be.'

'Well – cheerio then – father.'

'Aye Johann – cheerio.' Then he laughs; a wry, sad laugh, and wipes his chin. 'And come the revolution lassie – tak the silver and bring it hame.' Then he stands up, draws himself up to his full height, which isn't much over five feet two, and says, 'I'll carry that kist fir ye – it's on my road.'

My sister, Jemima wants to say a hundred words to me but can't get one to come out of her mouth. Her bottom lip keeps quivering and tears spill down her cheeks. 'The bed'll be cold,' is all she manages before running out the door and off to her work.

Mother has said good-bye to many bairns. I'm just another one. And it's washing day and she likes to get started early. 'Yer big sister wanted to come but the bairn'll be keeping her nae doot. Well, cheerio then Johann,' she says, shaking my hand. 'Yer faither is carrying yer kist. It's on his way.'

And that is that.

Leith Walk is a golden river and I am sailing up her – not going to the shoe shop, not running an errand, not hanging about outside the public house to plead for Thomas Blackie to please come home. Thomas Blackie is right next to me and I am his wee lassie getting a collie buckie up the wide Walk to sit in a golden field and gorge myself on strawberries and sing along when father and the other workers sing in the fruit bushes;

Wi' a hundred pipers an a' an a'
Wi' a hundred pipers an a'.

And maybe he remembers that time too, or maybe I am humming the tune, but there we are, me, the young lady in my Sunday best, practically skipping to miss the cracks on the pavement and father swinging my kist and singing;

O it's ower the border awa, awa,
It's ower the border awa, awa,
We'll on and we'll march tae Carlisle Ha,'
Wi its yetts, its castle an a' an a'.

His voice and the way he belts out the words, never heeding the looks of the toffs up on Princes street, keeps singing in me for a long time afterwards. When we reach the railway station we're caught up in the hub-bub of folks rushing here and there; guards whistling, porters pulling wooden chests on hand-carts, people waving hankies. Father has rarely if ever been in the Waverley railway station and he looks like a fish out of water. He sets my kist at his feet and sighs, his hands now plunged into the baggy pockets of his threadbare jacket and his head lowered.

'That's the train,' I shout, pointing to the platform where a huge steam train is receiving passengers. Father hauls my kist up the high train step, sets me down on a seat by the window in an empty carriage then places the kist on my lap. He looks uncomfortable, being dressed for his work as a market gardener. He shakes my hand quickly, says 'cheerio then,' turns round, hurries out of the carriage and jumps off the train. I wave to him before he's swallowed up into the jostling crowd.

And I'm ready to burst into tears there and then when a lass of about my own age comes into the carriage and sits down opposite me. She too clutches at her wooden kist that's straddled across her lap. She too waves her gloved hand at great speed at a small, thin looking man on the platform who waves back at her. When he's lost in the jostling crowd she, like me, looks fit to cry. I watch her bottom lip quiver. So I smile at her quickly, and she smiles back. The guard's whistle blows and the tears filling up behind my eyes don't spill down as I fear. But there's a flutter of butterflies in my stomach. We're off! The train, with a good deal of grating, squealing, puffing and clanking, leaves the station.

I am fourteen years old and I'm on my way.

3

Every ten minutes or so the train pulls into a busy station and even more girls with kists pile onto the train. Then there's more hankie waving and eye dabbing. The ticket inspector comes round, dressed in a very smart dark blue suit and hat. The girl opposite me fumbles so much with her ticket it slips out her fingers and falls onto the floor. She looks as though she's going to burst into tears again. I place my kist on the empty seat beside me then bend to fetch it up for her.

' Oh! Thanking ye so much,' she says. When the ticket inspector goes, wishing us a grand day and a rare view of the hills, she bites her lip then blurts out; 'Sadie Macdonald,' and she thrusts out her hand.

I shake it and feel how she's trembling. 'Johanna Blackie,' I say and at exactly the same time we both blurt out; 'very pleased to meet you.' Which makes the both of us laugh out loud. Sadie flops back on the seat, looking much the better for the laughter.

'Thon's a bonny kist,' she says.

'Oh. Thank you. So is yours as well.' I am right glad to have someone to talk to. I forget I am leaving behind everything and everyone I've ever known.

'Oh thank you. Mother got it made by the carpenter. I didnae think it would be so heavy. My legs have turned numb. Is yours heavy?'

I guess she's got more in her kist than I do. I shake my head. 'Not very much.'

'Oh, well, my legs have gone tae sleep. It's the bed sheets, they're that heavy. Mother says I had to take them for when I get a hoose o' my ain. But they're right heavy these bed sheets.' She squirms about and I think maybe she should put the kist on the floor or on the empty seat next to her but I don't say anything. She carries on speaking. 'We'll be met. D'ye think? Mother says we should be met. D'ye think we'll be met?'

'I think we'll be met,' I say, hoping so. 'The agency says we'll be met. And they says if we're no met tae follow the map. Did you get a map?' I bring out the piece of paper the lady in the 'Agency for the Engagement of Domestic Servants' gave me. On it she had drawn a map to the house – Grange House. It was two miles out of the pretty village of Comrie. She'd said to follow her map should the transport fail to arrive. Sadie strains forward over her kist to look at my map then she shakes her head sadly.

'That's no my hoose, we're no in the same hoose.' She seems crest-fallen. I am astonished how her pretty face shifts from summer to winter in an instant. As I fold up my precious map her sun comes out again. 'But you and me are close, Johanna,' she says. 'Maybe we can go oot walkin' on the holidays? If you like? We could go and paddle in the river? Maybe we could get a boat? They give us a holiday on Victoria Day. Mother says there's a grand river. The Earn, she says. That's its name. Aye, we did rivers at the school. Aye, there's the Forth, the Tay, the Clyde and the Earn. Did you know that?'

I shake my head. I can't remember if Miss Macdonald taught us the names of rivers. 'Oh, you have bonny dark hair,' she bursts out, 'not mousey like mine. Oh, I don't know anybody. Do you, Johanna?'

***

I stood against the door jamb, grateful for the cool air across my neck. It was the hour I expected my husband home. Half past five and still I stood there, lost in memories. A quarter to six and I was still there, peering anxiously up the street. The stew would spoil. I went inside and set the table though no two plates in the scant cupboard were the same.

He came home at seven. Being fresh married I could hardly complain. I heated up the stew and served him. 'Eat up Willie,' I said. He stared at the table all set and spread with the clean tablecloth I had brought with me in my kist. You'd swear he'd never sat down at a clean table to eat a meal.

'What's wrong, Willie?' I asked him.

'Nothing at all, Mrs Lockhart,' he replied, picking up his fork. We ate in silence.

'Not good enough for you then?' he said when he'd finished the stew and pushed his plate back. He was looking around him now, taking in the way the place shone, or maybe the way everything was re-arranged.

I laughed nervously and hurried to bring the bowls of bread and butter pudding to the table, thinking how hard he had kissed me the night before. How he had been rough and pulled at my hair. How when he pushed his urgent lips down over mine I smelled that trace of whisky. How he burrowed his whole self into me and all the while I felt like I was drowning in the reek of the public houses I'd stood outside, calling for father to come home.

Then how I had sobbed silently while he slept. How I had taken my hand and stroked his back and left it lying on his sleeping shoulder. My heart tugged back and forth, from the dreams of the past to this present. I was wed. I heard again the minister's words – honour and obey. More than anything I wanted to do my best, to make things work. To stop dreaming of what was gone. I wasn't the only one. The blasted war killed thousands of sweethearts, and as I had heard a hundred times, I just had to get on with it. I set the bowls down. Willie turned to me, then pulled my head to him, clutched my hair tight and kissed my mouth. 'I like a good pudding,' he said, leaving me breathless. We ate not speaking. The spoons clattered like bells. When he was done he sat by the fire and lit his pipe. But the smell of beer and whisky was in me now. Even the tobacco couldn't mask it. He's just celebrating being wed, I told myself, clearing the table the way I'd learnt to, without a sound.

Willie's wedding celebrations lasted weeks. The hovel he'd brought me to shone like a new pin. 'Do you not like it clean?' I asked him, the way he scowled at the windows I buffed up with vinegar. 'You can see through now.'

'Through to what, Johanna?' he said, then his scowl turned to a grin.

'I could plant some geraniums,' I said but by now his hands were pulling at my pinny.

'We dinny want nosy folks peeking in,' he pulled me to him, 'do we?'

I must have fallen on the first night. Or soon enough. I could hardly credit the notion. A bairn! I waited until my skirt wouldn't button up at the back before I told him. 'An heir,' Willie said, sweeping his hand grandly from the fire place to the front door. Then he winked and brought down his bowler hat from the peg. Another reason to celebrate. Another reason to sing in the street.

With a bairn growing inside me I knitted. My fingers flew over the pins as fast as Willie's over the neck of his fiddle. I started with the Christening shawl, then wee white vests, bootees, bibs. This bairn would be warm. This bairn would be well dressed. And the truth was, I couldn't do to have idle hands. Idle hands twisting in my lap just brought the clamouring thoughts in, the ones that said I had made a terrible mistake. I clicked the needles hard, drowning the thoughts.

But the thoughts came anyway. They grew louder. Every night there was drink on his breath. And there was me, fondly and foolishly imagining he was bent over a desk mending watches all day. I began to doubt that. I knitted faster. I began to doubt everything. The neighbours sniggered after I walked past in the street. If they saw me in church they cast their eyes to the holy ceiling. I felt a laughing stock. I knitted like a woman demented. And in secret I took up paper and the ink pen. Feeling like a thief in the night, I wrote quickly without hardly thinking…

76 Cobbler's Wynd
Haddington
5th May 1919

My dearest James

They are not sure you are dead. Why did you not come for me? I read in the newspaper that some of the 51st Battalion went missing. So many unaccounted for, I read. Some may be wandering the hills and byways of France, forgetting who they are. That's what they're saying. So many dead on the Western Front. Your regiment suffered great losses, oh James. Then if you are dead your loss is far greater than mine. Forgive me but James, I have made a terrible mistake. I am married and after only a few hours, if I am honest, and let me be that with you, I knew I had chosen badly. I try now to stop my heart from breaking. I feel I am wrapping it up with bandages to hold it in place.

But there are two young speckled thrushes that come and sit on the window ledge, so tame. They are hungry like the rest of us. I leave out crumbs for them. You showed me the mallards and the coots. You said you loved to lie in bed at night, your arms sore with rowing, and listen to the owls calling. One time you said it sounded as if they were calling my name.

Now I have much time to remember you and though in the few and precious times we had together I was too full of joy and youth and love to notice, now as I revisit you, over and over, I think how often you spoke of birds. How you knew the names of them.

I am a bird in a cage and no longer have the heart to sing and perhaps I would die inside without the song I keep alive for you.

Your dear friend
Johanna

Hurriedly, and with shaking hands, I wrapped the letter in tissue and placed it, like others I had written, in my kist. Then I picked up my knitting, my heart racing, fingers trembling and my cheeks flushed red.

'Ye've fine hands, Johanna,' Willie said, staring at my growing pile of tiny clothes. He was impressed with my skills, I could tell. 'But the wee laddie'll no be needin' all these.' He pinched my cheek. 'Less playing the needles and more playing yer husband here, eh?' He laughed, tapping his fingers the length and breadth of his waistcoat.

'Ach, away ye go,' I said, shaking my head, knitting faster. But the night would come. I'd put the knitting by, the wee bib or tiny vest. And many's the night I sobbed my pillow wet but, afterwards, I'd rest my hand on his back, trying to pour goodness into him. I wanted to believe he was a good man. I wanted to believe I had made a good bed.

Winter was coming. I spread coats on the bed. And my belly was growing.

4

'You're a Lockhart now, woman,' he said, tapping my swollen belly with his bow. Then he lifted his fiddle to his chin and played a jig for me and the bairn that was in me. It was early spring and the first daffodils had come up in the back green. There were primroses too. Aye, Haddington was bonnie, it was true. Willie sat on the step at the back door and for once I let off cleaning, washing and cooking. And I let go of the dark thoughts. The thoughts that tugged at me, saying I never should have married William Lockhart. Maybe it was me at fault? What did I know anyway of men, short of a handsome boatsman, a drunken father and pernickety butlers?

So I untied my pinny, hung it on the peg at the back door and stepped outside to the back green. There wasn't just me there. A lot of the neighbours had drawn around 'the mannie wi' the fiddle' as they called him, and even a few matrons in their long starched aprons came out to take the air, and a wee bit tune.

When Willie played the fiddle I let go bothering about my chores. I even let go bothering about his watchmaker's shop and the precious little watches that seemed ever to be made in it – and the brown envelopes he threw to the fire and the smell of beer on him. My feet tapped on the stone step, like they had a mind of their own.

I felt the bairn under my ribs kick, as though it was dancing to its father's music. I rubbed my belly and thought of how we'd dander together up the hill I could see from the kitchen window. We'd go for a picnic, a family outing. And Willie would play and the bairn would sing.

He switched to a faster jig. 'Come on lass – dance. It's guid for the bairn.' Willie's eyes were gleaming. Some of the neighbours were up and kicking their heels to 'hey Johnny Cope'. I shook my head. The thought of it! Who'd ever dance with a ripe belly? I liked watching my husband's long fingers race over the neck of his fiddle; me leaning on the door jamb, my stomach straining under my frock. I told myself then I was lucky. Mr James Melville couldn't play the fiddle. I felt a jab under my rib cage. James was dead in France, buried in a field of poppies. I shook my head and gulped at the sweet air. I patted the great mound of my belly then twisted the thin ring on my finger.

With the early evening sun warming my face I didn't want to go back into the dim pokey house. A man shouted for Scots Wha Hae. Willie played, his foot stamping wildly on the flagstone. He was never so happy when it was just the two of us, indoors, supping broth. Willie beamed and rocked his whole body back and forward with the music. The men joined in with the song. To hear them you'd think William Wallace himself was amongst them;

Scots, wha hae wi' Wallace bled,
Scots wham Bruce has often led
Welcome tae yer gory bed
Or tae Victorie!

The men sang loud, the children clapped, the womenfolk hummed along and when Willie came to the freedom verse he couldn't contain himself but hugged his fiddle to his breast and sung with them at the top of his voice;

Wha for Scotland's King and law
Freedom's sword will strongly draw
Freeman stand or freeman fa'
Let him on wi' me!

Willie's eyes were closed, his face flushed and there he was, on the peak of some dark Highland mountain. His fine fingers grasped the neck of the fiddle. Who was this man I had married? This man full of music, stories and communist philosophies. Full of swagger and bravado. A man who could laugh one minute, weep the next. 'If only *my* man played the fiddle,' a woman close to me said, sighing and nudging the man next to her. But there was joy in her complaint and in his laugh, like a shared secret. I saw how he leant close to her and ruffled her hair. I heard how he whispered, and hardly in a low voice either, that at least he could play her. The pair of them giggled, glanced at me then glanced away. I ignored them, folded my arms tight and watched my husband. He was lifting his fiddle back to his neck, ready for another tune. He scraped the bow over the strings. The way the music floated; rising, falling then swelling brought the memories rushing in. I only had to close my eyes for a moment and I was back, unmarried.

After church I tell Grace I want to walk on my own for a bit.

Grace is the parlour maid and my friend. She looks at me and shakes her head. 'I'll be just fine,' I say, then I hurry off. The folks in their Sunday finery glide away from the church. You can't tell the servants from the gentry on Sundays. I told Grace that. 'Yer havering, Johanna,' she told me. 'Of course you can.'

I smooth my skirt down over my hips and tug the hem of my jacket. I tilt the brim of my hat down and walk hurriedly past the clusters of people. They like to chatter after the service. But not me. He'll be down at the river. He said he would be there. I feel a flutter in my breast. Is it brazen of me to go alone? I almost turn round then. My steps falter. Perhaps I should take Grace along as chaperone? Glancing back I see her vanish into the carriage; the one the big house sends down for the servants. So it is decided then. Fate. I hurry away, heedless of the two mile walk I'll have later. Soon I can see the blue drape of the river, a haze beyond the green of the field. There are boats out and so I lift my skirts and run. White butterflies flit about me. I want to laugh out loud.

When I get down to the river bank I'm panting. There he is, studying the river, a strong hand lifted to shield his eyes. Even from the back I know him. I press my own hand to my chest, to try and slow my breath. 'Hello,' I say. I am surprised how steady my voice sounds. He turns around quickly. For a second it looks as though he doesn't know me. I tip back the brim of my hat and smile nervously. Why would he know me? He must take a hundred girls boating.

'Hello,' he says. He is smiling, a broad smile. He flits his eyes to where his boat is tethered. 'It's a fine day for a boat trip, is it not?'

'Aye,' I say, though I had meant to say yes. I take a step towards him. 'It is a very fine day indeed.' I try to speak like a lady. But if he remembers me from the Victoria holiday he'll know I'm in service. I remember Grace saying a man such as James Melville will be going to the university. 'Don't think he's just a boatman, Johanna,' is what she said. Don't go getting your hopes high just to have them dashed, is what she meant. But I could be a teacher, I told her. Miss Macdonald, my teacher in the school, said I showed great promise. I was, she said, a great letter writer.

'You're a servant, Johanna,' Grace reminds me.

'It's sixpence,' he says.

I nod. Perhaps mother won't mind going short. Then he laughs. 'Usually.' And he stretches his hand out to me. 'But not for you. It's Blackie, isn't it? Miss Blackie? You were here before. I remember you.'

I nod. I wish he would call me Johanna. 'I'm happy to pay,' I say and shake his hand.

He smiles. My eyes travel him. I notice his wide forehead. I think it is an intelligent forehead. I notice how jet his hair is, like mine. And his shining eyes seem to talk to my eyes. I thought they were blue, now I'm not sure if they are green or blue. 'I didn't think you'd come back,' he says, and smiles, as though he is glad I have.

I nod. I don't know what to say. I am utterly happy he remembers me from when us servant girls had our day's holiday on Victoria Day. So he knows I am no lady of leisure. I feel a weight of pretence fall from me. Then I take his offered hand and feel its warmth, like such goodness. As he guides me onto the boat I feel him touch the small of my back.

James Melville rows me up the river and all the way I am dissolving but somehow manage to speak. Once I begin words pour out of me. I am flabbergasted how much I speak. I tell him about the work in Grange House, and the many fires I set and that I will soon turn seventeen and how back home in Leith father is a market gardener and mother likes to keep the house clean and how she bakes scones and how we like to walk together in Princes Street Gardens. Mother and I have walked all of once in Princes Street Gardens and scones are a rarity. Of course I don't tell him that. 'Does he know Edinburgh?' I ask, tilting my head. 'Does he know of the lovely Princes Street Gardens? And the castle on the rock?'

'I hope to,' he says and looks at me as if he sees me completely, as if he is imagining he and I walking in the rose gardens of Edinburgh. He rows the boat so effortlessly. The rhythm of the oars and the sound of the water work like rose petals opening in my breast. Don't stop, I want to say. Let's go down this river for ever, you and me.

'University,' he says. So Grace was right. 'Of course, there's the war to go to first. A man has to.' He narrows his eyes and gazes at me as if he wants me to say – no – a man doesn't have to.

'Then, when that's done with, I'll study. I want to learn as much as I can. I want to see the world. And of course,' he leans forward and I think he might kiss me. 'I do want to marry. I do want to find me a good woman.'

I stare into my lap. My gloves have become wrinkled. The hem of the right-hand glove is frayed. 'I have to go,' I blurt out. 'They'll be…looking for me.'

'Of course,' he says, dipping in the oars and pulling back the river. The sunlight bounces off the water. 'It is beautiful here, isn't it, Johanna?'

I nod, and look at him. 'I mean, everything,' he says, 'the peace, the river, you… everything. I wish I could hold this moment. Stop the clocks.'

***

I saw the flush on Willie's face and guessed he could sing and play for hours. But it was time for supper. I had started the habit of giving him a cup of tea and a sweet biscuit every night at this time –and I warmed the bed with a bottle and tried to keep him out of the public house. It was time we were in and my back was sore now. I stepped forward and tugged gently at his sleeve. But my husband was having none of it. 'Wheesht woman, the party's hardly got started.' Then someone called for a Burns song.

'I'll gie you 'Ca' The Yowes,' Willie said, turning to where I was standing behind him. He winked at me. 'Thon's my favourite song, Johanna,' he said. Then the whole company fell silent and there was my Willie, turning from patriotic fever to flowing tears in an instant.

Ca' the yowes, tae the knowes

Ca' them whaur the heather grows -

The wee mite inside me kicked and I tipped my head to the side with the rest of them. When he was done he sat himself down on the back step and looked up at me, tears misting his eyes, 'if I die afore ye, sing it when they carry my box oot.'

I could only nod. What a request. And me too shy for the singing. But I smiled then bent towards him. 'Away in with you, fiddler man, in and get a cup o' tea.'

The neighbours drifted away after that. The sun was going down and there was a chill come into the air. And no one liked leaving a fire too long untended. Willie groaned and I helped him up. Then I hurried into the house and put the kettle to whistle on the fire but Willie, though he had followed me into the house, was of a different mind. A party had started in him and it was too early to stop.

'That music puts the heart in no mood for tea,' he said, sucking at his pipe and not sitting down. I wanted us to sit by the fire and talk about names. I'd stoked the fire and the room was warm. If it was a girl I wanted to give her mother's name. Would Willie raise an objection to that? But I had no chance to ask. 'You sup on your tea,' he said, putting on his bowler hat.

'Willie, stay. Don't go. I get lonely when you're out a' the time. And I don't know folks in Haddington. They look down on me. They do. Willie? There's nobody tae talk wi, Willie.'

'Wheesht woman – ye've a bairn kicking away right inside you. I'm just taking a wee walk.'

'Then I'll walk with you, Willie.'

'Not in your condition you won't.'

'Willie – please. I've been on my feet walking all day, cleaning and washing. Another wee walk won't kill me. Willie! Willie – what d'ye think about the name Jane?'

I didn't know what Willie thought about the name Jane.

He was gone.

5

One potato, two potato, three potato, four,
If you are baby number three gang oot the door.

I don't know what number I am. I run up the dim stairwell to tug at mother's heavy long skirt and ask her. 'Ma seventh,' she says, pressing her face down close tae mine, 'so watch yersel.' The same hot sour smell I know from faither, and her head swaying like a rag doll.

When I tell them down on the street they won't let me play peevers. 'Johanna rides a broomstick way up in the sky, she's got a black cat an' a pointy hat an' kens hoo we're a' going tae die.'

'Well, tell them ye're number two,' mother says, sucking her teeth and smoothing my smock down, 'for you're that as well, and that's a right re-spect-able number tae be.'

I am Jane Scott's seventh child. Thomas Blackie's ninth. Their second. Or their joint fourteenth.

Mother has a hard tongue on her but respectable is a word she likes. She makes it sound the best thing in the world – next to strawberries from Liberton. I make the ghostie shadows on the wall turn to fairies by saying Liberton and respectable. The girls in the street give me the peevers tin when I tell them I am baby number two and I have tasted strawberries and sat in a field in the sun and our family is respectable. I skite the shoe-polish tin over the pavement, willing it not to land in the chalk box marked seven. 'Coz seven's a witch,' they chant, 'and witches get burnt.'

***

Wee Jane Scott Lockhart was born on the 10th May 1920. Same year as the Communist party, Willie said. She was a bonnie wee thing with curly fair hair and a cherub of a face. The clothes I'd knitted fitted her just fine. I wasn't so lonely after Jane was born. But the house was even more cramped. And no amount of scrubbing would ever make it a proper home. The ceilings were too low, the place too damp and the windows that small precious little light came through, no matter how much vinegar I gave them.

Willie's sister Clara, now, her house was a very different kettle of fish. She lived in a grand stone house that stood by itself up near the church. There were rooms upstairs, rooms downstairs, a garden with apple trees in it, willow pattern crockery, fine walnut furniture –and samplers of the scriptures on every wall. After Jane was born Clara made it a habit to invite us for afternoon tea on a Sunday. Though she made it quite clear she was, 'doing her Christian duty.'

God is the Head of this Household
The Silent Listener at Every Conversation

was embroidered in fine red and gold twist on a dark blue background. *God* was sewn in gold cotton that shimmered when the sun slanted in, which was usually around three o'clock in the afternoon, the time we'd be bidden there. Jane slept under the table, wrapped in her blanket while I nibbled at Clara's Victoria Sponge and sipped at the tea in the fine bone china cup.

'A servant were ye?' Clara asked, dabbing her mouth with her large white linen napkin.

'Aye.'

'Must have been terrible living in these dock slums. Gordon Street down Leith he tells me. Heavens. No wonder ye went intae service.'

'Aye, ma'am.'

'Nae doot ye'll mak himself a tidy wife.'

'Aye.'

'Twenty six years old, he tells me?' She arched her dark eyebrows.

'Aye.'

'And he tells me ye have a grand talent for the stitching?'

'Aye.'

'Och, in the name o' the wee man, can ye no say ony mair than aye?'

'Aye. Aye, I can.'

'Weel?'

'It's – it's a right cold day – the day.'

'Aye, there's aye a lift off the sea in East Lothian. Better get used tae it. Mair tea *Mrs* Lockhart?'

'Aye, please. Thank you.'

I thought of Grace, the parlour maid back in the house in Trinity, and Sadie, God rest her soul, from my days in service up in Perthshire. How it had been so easy to talk to them. How I could think of a hundred things to say to them. And I thought of dear old Baxter, the cook in Trinity, and her jokes. She I could prattle away to. And to James I could have told my every thought and dream. Now I sat between the samplers and the potted plants, mute as if my tongue had been cut. Clara sighed and sat back in her chair, bored or exasperated, I couldn't tell which. She picked up the brass bell that stood next to the tea-pot and clanged it loudly. I gasped at the racket and wee Jane cried for a moment, then fell back to sleep.

If the bell was supposed to rouse a servant that servant was napping. 'Blooming half-wit,' Clara said and clanged the bell again, so vigorously I thought the tight lace ruff around her wrist was going to burst.

Finally the parlour door creaked open and there, standing half in the shadow of the door and half in the dusty sunlight, appeared the summoned servant girl. She was maybe eighteen or older though it was hard to tell. At one moment her round large face wore the expression of a child, the next of an old woman. She had bulging eyes and a pasty face and features that seemed too big for her face. Strands of lank hair escaped from her old-fashioned grey bonnet. Her jaw hung down and her thick tongue lolled out the side of her mouth. I couldn't help staring at her.

'Babs!' Clara snapped, 'how mony times have I telt ye – when ye hear this bell ye are called and so must come. At once!'

'But miss, sorry miss, I was in the cludgy.'

'At once.'

'Aye then meestress,' the servant said. All this time she was pulling at her apron which had got itself twisted around her and rode half way up her bum. She tugged at it then bent her knees in a clumsy curtsey. 'Aye aye meestress,' she repeated, in a sing-song voice.

'Gie idiots frae the Asylum a guid hame Mrs Lockhart and look what I get!'

I didn't know what to say. I gasped. I'd heard of the Asylum. Everybody had. Father's stories had been full of mouth-foaming lunatics who pressed their bulbous noses up against your window when you were fast asleep. Now here I was, face to face with a real lunatic.

'Right lassie,' Clara commanded, gesturing sharply to the items before her, 'tak the tea things ben the pantry and deal wi' them wi'oot breaking onything. And tell that Katie lump, maister's due his bath the night so he'll be needing fresh hot water.'

There was more than one! I pictured a whole gang of lunatics in the basement, pawing at the bars on the windows. Babs stood staring at the table, still fumbling with her pinny and drooling as she gaped at the remainder of the sponge cake. 'Aye meestress,' she said and clomped up to the table in her big rubber boots. I reached out to stack the plates but Clara stayed my hand.

'Ye are no a servant noo,' she snapped. 'As ye see, I hae my ain.'

So I wrung my hands together in my lap under the table while Babs, humming 'Onward Christian Soldiers,' stacked the tea plates onto a tray with a great deal of clattering.

'Wit a blooming din. Ye are like an elephant in a china shop. Mrs Lockhart here could teach ye a thing or two. Servants should be seen and not heard – and preferably not seen very often – is that not so Mrs Lockhart?'

I nodded and didn't know where to look. Willie, already stuffing his pipe with tobacco and seated at the fireside, paid no heed to all this, 'women's business.' I am ashamed to say I squirmed when suddenly Babs thrust her hand out, a big sweaty thing, right under my nose. 'Pleased tae meet ye Mrs Lockhart,' she said, so friendly and me so uncharitable.

'Oot!' shouted Clara. 'Servants dinnae hob-nob wi guests. Now gether up they tea things and quick march, oot! Oot afore I take the stick tae ye!'

Suddenly the fine stone house, with its leafy potted plants, red velvet drapes and China ornaments, embroidered scripture everywhere and loud chiming grandfather clock, seemed eerie. Then wee Jane, under the table, started to cry.

6

I am fourteen. I have a lot to learn.

'If you do see a Balfour while you're going about your work,' says Lizzie solemnly, 'be sure to curtsey.' Lizzie waits at the table and knows so much more than I do.

'How?'

'Right foot neatly in behind the left,' Lizzie replies, demonstrating the move with a good twenty pins in her mouth. It's Sunday afternoon. We're in our attic room and she's busy making herself a new pinny. 'Then doon ye go, quick, wi' yer head tilted doon, just a wee bit, then quick up again.'

I try it and she laughs. 'Jings Johanna, you're not in the music halls. Just a wee bit curtsey.' I try again, hoping I never find myself close up to the great Balfours. Curtseying is one thing. What will I ever find to say to them?

'Ye dinnae say anything,' Lizzie tells me sternly, jabbing pins into a hem. 'Most ye say is yes ma'am, no ma'am and that's just if they ask ye something.'

'Jings.'

'Aye, ye get used to it. And if ye come across a lady or gentlemen give them room Blackie. And turn yer head to the wall like ye're no there. And if ye have to carry a package tae the carriage for them mind walk a few paces back.'

I practise the curtsey every night in the bedroom and go over and over in my head the advice Lizzie gave me.

'Yes ma'am, no ma'am, yes sir, no sir.'

***

Being married, and living in Haddington, it was the company I missed most. Of course, a bairn was company, but not to tell your woes to. And Willie didn't tell me what he did at work. I tried to tell him what wee Jane had been up to, but after I'd gone on about how a tooth was coming through, or how she played away, rattling the spoons, then how she slept out in the back green, the words dried up. I didn't know what else to say. He didn't seem that interested. Perhaps that's why I wrote so often to James Melville. It almost didn't matter they were never sent. It gave me some solace to put pen to paper. It crossed my mind that I was going out of my mind. More than once, whilst gazing out the window, taking a breather in between my chores, I was convinced I spotted James Melville out on the street. Once I left the bairn sitting on the stone floor and dashed outside. I shouted his name. People turned and stared at me. I didn't care. 'James!' I cried and ran towards him, my heart pounding like a drum. But it was never him. I tugged a stranger's sleeve. He pushed me away, no doubt thinking I was a pick-pocket. I ran home, my cheeks burning with shame. And back in the dark little house the bairn was screaming. I picked up wee Jane and wept.

It was after that I gave myself a talking to. I was a grown woman now and here I was, carrying on like a love-sick lassie. 'Your mammy loved a soldier man,' I sang to wee Jane as I bounced her on my knee, 'but that was a long time ago, and your mammy is a soft hearted creature.' Jane pulled at my hair. '*Hickory dickory dock,*' I sang, '*the mouse ran up the clock…*'

If I could turn the talk to communism with Willie Lockhart, then I'd put a brand to the fire. Then he'd punch the air and talk revolution. He'd poke into his copy of the Daily Worker, pointing to his heroes of the day, and I vowed to read it, but there was never time. 'Watches,' I said, because I wanted to keep him in the house after dinner, 'tell me how you make something as fine and as small as a watch.'

'Well now, mither,' he said, because after Jane was born we switched to that. He called me mither. I called him faither. 'Mither,' he said, 'ye need fine long fingers fir tae mak a watch.' And he stretched his fingers out, turning them back and forth. 'And a watchmaker needs a guid feel for the workings, right at the pads o yer fingers. It's nimble work.' He brought out his own pocket watch, flicked it open then snapped it shut. 'It's a right fine trade,' he said, pocketing his watch with a flourish, 'tae be a watchmaker.'

'We need shoes for the bairn,' I said, catching him and his fine trade and his mood, 'for the winter.'

He punched his finger – his long slim finger – to some man in a cloth cap pictured in his newspaper. 'There's men with no bread, mither, and you talk o shoes.'

'You've money for drink.' It blurted out from me. I pursed my lips, willing the words to fall back.

Willie said nothing. He folded up his paper, in half, then pressed it into quarter, as though the heel of his hand was a smoothing iron. 'For the winter,' I said, quietly, looking into my lap.

'If Haddington was closer you can be sure I'd visit more often,' Grace said. Though she only managed a half day's visit once every couple of months I was right glad of the company. And I was grateful for the effort she made. Grace worked in Edinburgh and it was a good three hour journey out to Haddington, to say nothing of the fare. We always fell into talk of the old days. Grace had tried to ask me about Willie but what could I say? So I chatted on about wee Jane, then we'd fall to reminiscing. 'Remember the day we went boating?' I said, and Grace nodded and smiled. She ate my shortbread. She sipped my tea. She dandled the bairn on her lap. She let me dream, and agreed when I said how handsome he was, our strong boatman.

'And what kind of folks are they, in Haddington?' she asked me, changing the subject, blowing away the past and pulling me into the present.

'Not like us,' I said.

Sometimes, when I walked along the street, pushing wee Jane in the barrow, I saw a huddle of women leaning in doorways, their arms folded and shawls drawn tight around their shoulders. I felt their eyes follow me, measuring the cloth of my skirt, the swell on my stomach, the way I wore my hair. I caught snatches of their gossip. It fluttered like pine-needles in the wind. How I was a Blackie, and weren't they a bad poor lot, the Blackies? From a slum in Leith no less. How fifteen folk lived in one room and never washed in the Leith slums and TB was rife. How I had been a servant, liked rubbing shoulders with my betters and here I was, doing just that with the Lockharts in Haddington, no less. How I could think myself lucky – coming into the Lockhart clan and the good town of Haddington. Then, when I was far enough away from them, but near enough to catch the murmur of their voices, how there was a lot I didn't know about the old rogue Willie.

Old?

So I asked him.

Clara was at least forty. There were times I heard her refer to herself as Willie's wee sister! 'Or am I tae be your big sister noo Willie, let me ken,' she said, laughing when she thought I couldn't hear.

'Did ye lie to me, Willie?'

'Lie Johanna? Wit a thought!'

'You're not coming up for thirty five at all, are ye Willie Lockhart?'

'Fighting in the Highland Light Infantry puts years on a man Johanna. You should have seen the thin tasteless gruel they served us. No food for a man. Now the great pity is, you were not wi' us. Aye, we should have had you in the mess Mrs Lockhart. Then we would have kept our looks. Now, did I tell ye Mrs Lockhart, you are very handy with the stews and the soups and the rice puddings. A dab hand in fact.'

'And the custard,' I added, because he was always saying that was his favourite.

'Oh aye, and the custard.' He smacked his lips. 'The pity is big sister Clara can't cook like you,' and he winked at me and placed his hand across the mound of my stomach. I glanced down. For all his faults he did have fine hands.

I had to laugh. It was true about Clara's cooking. When we went there for dinner on a Sunday after church the meat was as tough as old boots. I could hardly swallow the food thinking about Babs and Katie drooling over it down in that filthy kitchen and them thinking nothing of dropping it on the floor and arranging it back on the plate.

'Well, I am glad you like my cooking,' I said, blushing suddenly. I still felt so young and inexperienced. Even with the feel of his hand pressed over my swollen stomach I felt shame.

'A laddie,' he said, taking his hand away. 'I'll call him William.'

But he was wrong. It was another girl, so we called her Williamina.

7

Us bairns are frightened of Coconut Tam.

Coconut Tam stands with his poor hunchy back, at the corner of Constitution Street with his wee stall of coconuts, calling out – 'cocynits, cocynits, a penny the bit, cocynits'. I see him dancing on the wall in the flickering shadows at night too and I don't want a coconut to chew because I might get a hunchy back. It's supposed to be a treat and mother has the brown hairy strips laid out on the kitchen table. Jemima takes hers but when I say how I don't want a hunchy back mother slaps me hard behind the knees. 'I'll gie ye hunchy back ye ungrateful wee bisom.' I have to stand in the corner. Even when father comes home and falls asleep in his chair I still have to stand. 'Teach ye tae think ye're ony better than onybody else,' mother says, and still I stand even though I cry buckets and sob how I *will* eat the coconut. I want to be best friends with Cocynit Tam, I wail. It's dark before she sends me to bed. No supper. Not even a blackened crust.

I was used to a lot of folks in a small space. Mother always said how that was the best way to heat a damp house. Now with Jane and wee Williamina that pokey house in Haddington grew livelier, what with the noise of babies crying and waking in the night and the stench of dirty nappies and them girning for food.

'Will ye wheesht and gie a man peace!'

'She'll no understand ye, Willie. The wee lassie needs tae exercise her lungs, that's all.'

'No when a man's sitting doon tae his denner. I've been working a' day and last thing a man needs is bairns screaming soon as he gets in the door.'

'Were ye working all day, Willie?' I asked, my voice shaking.

'Meaning what?' A trickle of gravy ran down his stubbled chin.

'Meaning – how is it doing? The shop? Do you have plenty customers?'

The bairns stopped screaming. Jane sat on the floor with her thumb in her mouth and Mina was silent.

'Plenty customers. More than I need.' Willie jabbed a potato. 'You should see the folks running to have Mr Lockhart repair their watch. You should see the old men with their pocket watches wanting me to fix the hour hand, or clean out the workings. And poor as church mice half o' them. Breaks my heart to see them, and to think o' them going about with their watch on a fine chain and the watch no keeping time. So – aye – plenty customers. But no' always the paying kind!'

Willie looked pleased with himself and chomped noisily. Just then the bairn toppled over and banged her head on the side of the table. She let out an almighty holler.

'Come tae me hen,' Willie said, bending to pick up his namesake. Immediately the bairn stopped yelling and I couldn't help but smile to hear my husband, the watch-maker, sing to his daughter:

Hickory dickory dock
The mouse ran up the clock.

Then wee Jane crawled over and hoisted herself up on his trouser leg.

'Me too,' she called out, pulling at his trousers, 'me, song, me.'

So he lifted her onto his other knee and bounced her up and down. Now the two of them were grinning like daffodils in the spring and squealing with glee as father sang:

I love Jenny over and over
I love Jenny in the clover;
I love Jenny and Jenny loves me

That's the lass that I'll gang wi'.

'We've a fine wee family,' I said, wanting it to always be like this. I even joined in with his song. I wanted to trust him but I'd seen the brown envelopes. I'd turned folk away from the door, the ones who came knocking saying Mr Lockhart owed them money – or Mr Lockhart promised to deliver their watch and where was it? Or Mr Lockhart is late with the rent.

'Grand,' Willie said. But of course the song would come to an end. There was a limit to his patience and to how many times he'd humour Jane with her, 'again, again, again!' Then it would be on with the black bowler hat. On with the muffler to keep his neck warm. His hand will jingle coins in his pocket. The door will creak open, a draught of cold air will rush in then the door will slam and Willie Lockhart is gone.

'Where's faither?' wee Jane asked when suddenly the singing was over and the wee house quiet.

'Knocking round the houses to get watches to mend,' I lied.

Then I would sing them to sleep, tucking them up under coats and blankets in the little bed at the foot of our bed.

Bluebells, dummie dummie shells
Evie ivy O-over!

It wasn't that many years ago I was a bairn myself, though it felt another lifetime.

Evie, ivy, over…

Me and Jemima playing with mother's kist, making it a bed for the dolls we don't have but imagine we do. Until the day Mother makes us one. She twists an old rag about the neck of a wooden spoon, and draws the face on the spoon with a lead pencil.

I love that dolly. I call her Victoria because that's the grandest name I know and it comes from the dead queen. Jemima calls her Fanny. It is the same doll with different names. Hours we spend, me and Jemima, playing with our wooden spoon dollies. We have to play together nicely. Mother's fast with the slapping, the back of the knees where it stings. So we share the dolly. Victoria and Fanny are always talking to each other;

I've got a fancy man, he lives in a castle,
And I've got a soldier man, he's away off to battle…

When we've done playing with the wooden spoon dolly we lie her down into mother's kist then hurtle pell-mell down to the street, two steps at a time.

Orangey, appely, damson jam, the bairns chant as they turn the rope. I run right in and jump high, *as fast as you can…* my skirt flapping up to my knees. I can skip and skip and never stop skipping. But sometimes we have to lower the skipping rope, to let a horse and cart go past. Some cart men sell pots and brushes. Some have bones. Other men don't have carts. These men just stand on the street, selling their wares. We're not allowed to go close to the knife-grinder with his oil-stone, sharp razors and bushy eyebrows in case he cuts our throats. And we've never to give cheek to a fishwife or we'll get slapped with a wet fish. We're always being told not to stand next to the bairns with the lice and Saturday night bath time always makes you cry. Mother has a bone comb and tugs it till I scream. Mother says she's damned if any respectable bairn of hers will go about the streets with a shaved heid.

Saturdays we get a sweetie; great round red gobstoppers that blows your cheeks out like a balloon. The trick is to see who can keep it the longest before it melts into a sliver of glass that cuts your tongue. Sometimes our father's got no money for a sweetie. Then it's a jammy piece or a stick of rhubarb stabbed down into a poke of sugar. But then some days he conjures a penny from his pocket, tosses it in the air, catches it and tells us to run off and buy a bottle of Sugarellie water.

Sugarellie water, black as the lum, gather up peens and you'll a' get some!

There are some boys, like the McPhees, who never get a sweetie, far less Sugarellie water. They run after me and Jemima, to get us to spit out our gobstoppers. I feel sorry for the bandy-legged McPhee boys with shaved heids, bare feet and shabby clothes and one time I give them my sweetie. They stand in a circle gawping. There's about ten of them, all boys. At least they look like boys with their shaved heids. They take turns at sookin' it. Geordie McPhee with the snotty nose gets my sweetie last. After he sooks on the sweetie he takes it out his mouth – a tiny red shiny thing – and hands it to me. I don't want it back, not with his snot and tongue all over it so I shake my head – and he kisses me on the cheek. At home I practise kissing Victoria, my wooden spoon dolly, and I whisper to Jemima that Geordie McPhee is my fancy man but if she dares tell anyone I'll slap her on the legs.

8

'Imagine my ain brother's wife a servant! And a laundry maid to boot!'

'In Edinburgh,' I said, trying to put some degree o' difference between Babs, Katie and myself. 'And I was happy,' I added.

If Clara picked up on the past tense she didn't show it. 'Well, lucky for you that's all behind you – and a watchmaker is certainly a fine thing.' Clara walked over to the mirror above the mantelpiece in the parlour and swept back a lock of dark hair that had fallen over her eye. I could hear Babs and Katie clattering in the dining room next door, setting the table for our Sunday dinner. Clara swept to the adjoining door, her black and stiff dress rustling with every step. She wore the same black dress every Sunday. It didn't go swish-swish, like I remember Miss Macdonald, my school teacher's dress did.

'Time, Mr and Mrs Lockhart, to go through,' she announced, as the clock chimed one o'clock. 'Snap-snap.' She lifted her strong jaw and extended her arm, as though bidding us to a grand ball. Willie and I rose from our chairs. Our footsteps echoed through the house in time to the ticking of the clock.

I can't eat my porridge.

In the church I can't even sing my favourite hymns. I'm going to see James

Melville. He's waiting for me down by the river. I have brushed my hair a hundred times. I have pinched my cheeks to put roses in them. Then the disappointment, as if the very heart in me is ripped from my breast. A footman from Grange House has come to tell us our half day holiday is cancelled. 'But....I have... an engagement,' I say, my voice rising with every word. It falls on deaf ears as us servants are ushered from the door of the church straight up into the waiting charabanc. There are fine guests arriving from London, we're told, and it's all hands needed on deck to make the house fit for them. I am frantic. The way Grace looks at me, she knows. 'Snap-snap,' the footman is saying. He is clapping his hands and looking exasperated. 'Women are so slow,' he says, shaking his head. I want to run away. Tears sting my eyes. The footman reaches out and grips his hand hard round my arm. 'Up with you now, missy,' he says, impatiently. I am falling. Dissolving. The horses neigh and the carriage jolts. I twist my neck to try and see the river. I see a blue ribbon in the distance, beyond the field.

'You know the rules,' Grace tells me, when we sit up late that night, in the servant's hall drinking tea, after scrubbing and polishing all afternoon. 'No courting.'

'But, he wants to marry me,' I say.

Grace knits her brow. 'Really?'

I blush and look down, can't meet the hard doubt in her eyes. 'He as much as said so.' I hold tight to the tea cup. If I break crockery it will be docked from my wages. If I am found courting I'll be sent home.

'Listen to me, Johanna. James is a handsome man, it's true. But you said it yourself, he is going to the university. He wants to see the world. And God help him, the poor man's going to fight the Huns. You and me, Johanna, we're cut from a different cloth.'

I stare into the brown tea. Poor, that's what she means. A few dark tea leaves cling to the inside of the cup. 'But I could go to the university,' I say, but know it isn't true. I want to read the tea leaves. I sip the last of the cold tea. I want to see James Melville in the leaves.

'Concentrate on your work, Johanna. You're a fine house-maid, and they want you down to help in the kitchen. Think of all you'll learn

Johanna. It'll put you in good stead. And we're lucky here. Grange House is respectable. Think of the reference.'

The grandfather clock whirs and the cogs click. The bells ring for midnight.

'Come on Blackie, we're up at six,' Grace says, patting me on the arm and setting her cup down. 'Time for the ferry man to ferry us over the river to sleep.'

'Aye,' I say, staring one last time into the dregs of my tea cup. The tea leaves clump together at the bottom, like a dark stain. The clock ticks loudly.

***

I hated those Sunday dinners with Clara. My children were whisked away and tended to by Babs and Katie and even if the food had been tasty I would have had trouble enjoying any of it for worry about my bairns.

'For heaven's sake Johanna, my servants might be dim-witted idiots but they're no evil monsters. Now calm yourself and eat up.'

I glanced down at my soup bowl and there, stamped grubbily on the side of the willow patterned dish, was Bab's lardy fingerprint that made me feel sick. As if that wasn't enough, floating about in the green liquid was one long lank hair.

'Wit is the matter, *Mrs* Lockhart?' Clara asked, slurping up her soup. She had this way of making mockery of the fact I was now Mrs Lockhart. 'Green split pea no good enough for you? No what you're used to – in the servant's halls?'

I lifted my napkin to my mouth, shook my head then smiled weakly at my sister-in-law.

Afterwards Clara read from the scriptures and Willie slept by the fire. The ordeal was never ending. After the bible reading Babs appeared to clear up and bring the tea through.

'Will I pour Mr Lockhart a cup o' tea meestress? Will I do that?'

'That will do fine, Babs.'

'Oh! I forgot the sugar mum.'

'Well go and get it you daft straw-heid. How many times have I telt ye to pit the sugar bowl on the tea tray?'

'Sorry mum. Very, very sorry mum. I won't do it again mum. Silly Babs. Babs is a right wee straw-heid.'

'Oh shut up and just bring the blooming sugar.'

Willie stirred then opened one eye. 'On the Sabbath too!'

'Aye and you can shut up an all.'

I opened my mouth to ask after my children but Babs was gone. Clara caught my eye darting to the cabinet. 'Aye Johanna, you may well look fir that cabinet has been in the Lockhart family for generations. It's quality. And many a fine letter was penned at that writing bureau too. If I needed to doubtless I could sell off thon cabinet for quite a fortune.'

I nodded, smiled weakly, and remembered my very first letter – written on a slate to my school teacher. 'Miss Macdonald. I love you,' I had written. I felt my face flush just thinking about it.

'And they velvet drapes. Grand aren't they? Castles have the same. Fine except when it comes to washing them.'

I nodded. I knew how arduous it was to wash velvet drapes. Though judging by the dust that puffed out when anyone brushed by I was sure Clara didn't bother. 'Haddington is that clean a place,' she said, perhaps seeing my eyes flit over her dusty drapes. 'No like Leith and Edinburgh where it's hard to breathe.'

I lowered my eyes. Clara went on. 'It is hard to breathe there, isn't it Johanna? They call it Auld Reekie. I hear folk have soot lining their lungs. Is that no the case?'

Maybe she was right. Trinity, my last place of work, had been a clean enough place and Perthshire before it had good pure air. But Leith? I shrugged. 'I don't know,' I said quietly.

'A lot of coughing, was there?'

'It was a long time ago. I think there was a lot of coughing – aye.'

'You see,' she trumped. 'The consumption. I told you. We're far better off here.'

Then, when Willie nodded off with his pipe still in his mouth Clara leant forward and said in a low voice, 'so, your wee hoose suits you fine still, does it?'

'Oh aye, very good ma'am.'

'Ye're not a servant now Johanna. How many times do I have tae tell ye, call me Clara.'

'Aye,' I said, feeling my cheeks flame, 'sorry, Clara. I will.'

She smiled at me in her lady of the house way and I tried to smile back. Still she was staring at me, then glancing at her brother, now snoring in the chair, then glancing meaningfully back at me. I nodded, coughed, said aye again, for no reason at all. I could hardly have turned to her and said, 'no Clara, the truth is, my wee house is a hovel in comparison. We have no such thing as a writing bureau or cabinet and have hardly enough money to keep the place warm. That wee fortune you mention could help feed the bairns and pay for the coal. For that's what happens when your money goes on drink – ye get coats on the bed, and water in the stew, and you close the curtains because you don't want the neighbours to see your man falling over.' I couldn't have said that.

'So, everything fine then?'

'The children,' I said, 'are a joy to me.'

Clara sat back and nodded then looked again at her brother. The way the pale afternoon sunlight slanted in and lit up his crumpled face gave him the appearance of an old man.

'Well, it's a good thing we have clean air in Haddington.' After that Clara said no more. She rose and went to fetch the children. I sat there in the parlour staring at my husband, the clock ticking loudly on the mantelpiece, the scriptures looming down on me; God my silent witness. I wrung my hands in my lap and wanted to cry. You'd think I would have known. I, with my own father reeling home drunk almost every night and me frightened to death he'd crush me as he fell. You'd think I of all people would have known.

I bit my lip and held back the tears that in the quietness of that parlour on a Sunday afternoon with the sun going down over the fine ornaments, threatened to spill down my cheeks. 'You went into service to get away from a drinking father,' I thought to myself, 'only to find yourself married to a drinking man. God help you.' I glanced up at the panel above the mantelpiece – **the Lord is my shepherd I shall not want.** There was some comfort in that, and in the sound of my children's light footsteps running in the hallway, and the cry of their high voices calling, 'mither, mither, mither!'

9

When Jane was two, and Willamina was one and a half, William was born; a boy this time so he too took his father's name. There was no question over that. But, foolish hearted woman that I was, I chose his middle name. James. I said it had to be James. 'Where's there a James in the family?' Willie said, not over fond of the name. So help me but I lied to him. Said I once had an uncle, a good man he was, and James was his name. So my first born son was Christened William James Lockhart. A sweet faced laddie with a twinkle in his eye and though a good bairn and never one for girning that wee house of ours became less and less the place for a man.

I saw the expressions of the women on the street. I caught enough snatches of their gossip as I went from shop to shop, searching for the cheapest cuts, buying second day bread, bruised apples, trailing all three bairns and trying to make Willie's few coins feed a family. 'There goes poor Mrs Lockhart. Look at her wi' a' they bairns. One falls aff the breest and there's anither in the pot. They never taught her the word no in Leith. Servants only ken one word – yes ma'am, certainly ma'am, yes sir!'

'They look down on me faither. Even your own folks look down on me. And they say there's a' sorts o' things about you I dinnae ken,' I said one night, as we sat there supping a thin lentil soup while the bairns played marbles with pebbles on the floor. Willie had had a few, I could tell, and it still daylight. I sighed. He was spilling my soup all over the clean table-cloth. My nerves were wearing thin. It had been one of these days where every shop keeper looked sorry for me, every person I passed on the street hushed in their gossip then picked up their wicked threads soon as I was past.

'Dinnae heed the gossips mother,' said he, waving his spoon like it was a magic wand, soup dripping on my table cloth. 'Dinnae heed them!' But I wasn't going to let it lie like I usually did. Him and the place were wearing me down. I was only twenty nine but felt ancient. And I'd found out, because Clara let it slip, that this drunkard I called husband was hardly the young thing he made himself out to be.

'Forty nine come his next birthday, and precious little gift he's getting frae me!'

'What did ye say Clara?'

'Aye, precious little. A pouch o' baccy if he's lucky. I invite you here oot o' charity and he says the meat's tough as old boots. I'll charity him!'

I could hardly hold my tongue. Soon as we were home I turned on him. 'Forty nine? Ye lied to me. For the love of goodness, you're forty nine. And here's me thinking you were ten years younger. What else is a lie?'

Scowling he splattered a spoonful of lentil soup on my good tablecloth. 'Wheesht,' he said, but I wouldn't be quiet.

'Oh aye,' I went on, not caring it's in front of the bairns, 'easy for you to sit there and pan me off, just like ye pan off your customers that come to the door wanting their watches back, just like ye pan off the tax man and the rent collector.'

'Wheesht woman, yea're getting hysterical. Just wheesht or I'll make ye – then you'll be sorry.'

'Then? I've been sorry for a long while now Willie Lockhart. I'm sorry I ever married ye. You're a drunkard, and a liar. You fooled me into marrying an auld man – and don't say you're not auld. Late thirties? Ha! Forty nine! That's what you are. Auld enough to be my faither. I canny depend on ye.'

'I says wheesht or I'll come over – aye – I'll come over and pour this soup ower yer heid!'

'You can't even stand up like a decent human being. Look at the state o' ye? Shame on ye and in front o' yer ain bairns. You're that drunk I can't bear it. How can you come in here at five o'clock drunk? Were you not at work? God gie me strength.' I got up from the table and left him staring into his soup bowl. I couldn't stand to look at him.

'I shays wheesht woman,' said he, banging his spoon on the table.

'Hud yer dirty tongue. Ye're a Lockhart now and it's high time ye learnt tae behave like one. And anyway – I'll huv ye ken, work is man's business. You just get on wi' woman's business and dinnae poke yer nose in aboot mine. And ma age,' the spoon clattered on the floor, 'is my ain business.'

I turned to look at him, disgusted. How could I have been so naïve? Did I know nothing of the world short of cleaning houses? Was I that blind I couldn't even tell a man's age? Willie thumped his fist hard on the table and sent my good bowl from my own kist to follow the spoon to the stone floor. It smashed. Jane screamed. Then he staggered to his feet, grabbed a knife from the table and waved it in the air. I dived to protect the bairns as Willie slumped to the floor, groaning and cursing. The knife followed everything else onto the stone floor.

Had there been any candle burning in me for this man it snuffed out then. I had seen this before, heard this before, had front seat at the concert of the drunkard show too many times. But even Tam Blackie didn't threaten us with a knife.

I gathered the children up and hurried them all through to the bed. 'Shame on ye, Willie Lockhart,' I sobbed, clasping the children tight. I knew how to carry three bairns at once. Wee Mina could talk by this time. 'What's the matter wi ma faither?' she said, pulling at my hair.

'That's what I'd like to ken,' I said, laying her into the bed and stroking her soft cheek. I fought to keep the trembling out of my voice. 'What's the matter wi' yer faither?'

Young Jane made her wee hands into fists and I swear the brave wee thing would have run through to where her faither lay, groaning on the floor, and would have punched him hard. But I tucked her in next to her sister and stroked their small heads and all the while rocked wee Jamesy in my arms. I found a song inside me for them that night, though never did I feel less like singing.

Aly bally aly bally bee, sitting on yer mammy's knee
Weeping for a wee baw'bee, tae buy some coulter's candy.

I had saved up a few shillings in a tin that I kept hidden. Domestic service had served me well. I knew how to make a small knuckle of beef go a long way – and something told me I'd be needing the saved shillings sooner rather than later.

Willie was on the drink, well into his cups, drunk night after night and all manners forgotten. Here was a man who sang his hymns in church on a Sunday with gusto and cursed like the devil Monday to Saturday. I prayed for the time every night when he would fall asleep. With three young bairns I tried to keep the peace, to get him into bed, to take his boots off and clean any mess he made. 'Show's yer paps, Johann,' he said, pawing at me. I pushed him away, almost glad he was drunk with the spirit willing but flesh so weak.

I turned away from him and made my voice a soft coaxing thing; 'away wi' ye faither, wheesht now and go to sleep.'

'Aye right then, mother.' Those were the good nights.

Then there were the nights when the drink stirred him hot, when his pawing would go on and on, his hard hands and groping fingers clammy on my body, insistent and him slurring, 'it's yer duty as a wife. Fine paps.' When I refused he'd get angry and beat the bed. 'Go ben and bring me the knife. Go on! Get it, so's I can kill you. Aye, I'm gonna kill ye!'

But he was always too drunk to go and get the knife himself.

'Wheesht now faither and go to sleep.'

I lived in fear that one day he would get that knife and it wouldn't be me he'd kill, it would be the bairns. Half the time he was that drunk he didn't know what he was doing. I wouldn't put it past him. Every breath I took was shortened with fear. The bairns too – I could see it in their eyes. When the front door opened and faither swung in a shadow fell over their faces. They stopped what they were doing. They cut their songs mid verse. They held their breath. Would faither be singing tonight? Would faither be falling down? Would faither dandle them on his knee?

It was the day after one too many drunken nights – him demanding the knife, me coaxing him to sleep, him demanding a wife does her duty, the reek of cheap beer and whisky making me sick, bairns screaming. The day after all that, when Grace came to visit, I couldn't help it but it all poured out of me. How I had been a fool. How he was much older than I thought. And a drunkard. And how he threatened us, night after night with the knife. Grace, the serious faced spinster, but my best friend, listened, her face turning pale.

'You are within your rights to go,' she said, her voice hushed and the two of us forever glancing over our shoulders as if the red-faced drunkard would come lurching in any moment. But he didn't. Grace had a job in the Overseas Club in Princes Street and often helped me out with a couple of shillings. Said if she had the room we could stay with her, but she only had the one room above the club and children weren't allowed. 'But your own mother will take you back,' she said, 'surely. For your own safety, and the bairns, you must leave him, Johanna. You must.' She pressed a sixpence into my hand. 'You hear me? You must.'

The next day my mind was made up. I tipped the contents of the tin onto the bed. I counted the money, my heart racing. There was enough to take me and the bairns on a horse-drawn bus to Leith, and a bit over for something to eat and a wee bit towards some rent for mother. I bundled up a few belongings in my kist, put as many clothes on the bairns' back as they could cope with and left.

Right glad was I to hear the click of the latch behind me. I breathed a sigh of relief and with the kist in one hand, wee Jamesy in the crook of my other arm and Mina and Jane holding my skirt I hurried along the back street praying I wouldn't bump into Clara or one of the Lockhart family. I was lucky and made it onto the bus, feeling like a fugitive. In the bus the children cried and the other travellers felt sorry for me.

'Lost your man in the war did you dear?' one woman said. I nodded, thinking of James, then quickly shook my head, not trusting myself to talk. My hands, like they had a mind of their own, kept pulling at my skirt. The bus felt airless. 'Damn shame,' the woman went on. 'He'll be at peace in thon fields in France now though. He'll be looking down on ye, aye, I ken. I ken all aboot it. Wit a waste. Aye, wit a waste o young blood.' I turned and gazed out of the window but still she went on. 'And you so young and bonny too.'

I sat on that horse drawn bus to Edinburgh with a stony face, rocking wee baby Jamesy and trying to cheer up Mina and Jane who wouldn't sit still. 'It's a bloody shame,' the woman on the bus went on; the woman who wouldn't shut up. I didn't want to talk to her but she talked anyway. 'I lost my ain brother, and my sister's boy, young Kevin. We even lost the postman and he had three bairns. They've all gone. It's a bloody tragedy.' I bounced wee Jamesy on my knee. Jane stood up on the seat and before I could pull her down she told the woman; 'our faither fell down on the floor. He's always falling down on the floor. He's not dead.' The woman on the bus turned quiet after that. As we approached Edinburgh she piped up again. 'Anyway, you bairns have a rare time playing in Edinburgh.' I turned my head and looked out of the window, hoping against hope they would.

Me and Jemima sling the old rugs over the line in the back green then punch till clouds of dust burst into the air.

One time we can't find the rug beater so we're handed a wooden spoon. There I am thudding away grand style before I notice it's my dolly, Victoria – and I've bashed her so hard her dress has come loose and falls off. She's just a thin wooden spoon and her face is drawn on spots and she's dead.

'Guess what I'm bashing wi?' I say to Jemima. Though she's a year older she's slower than me. I always understand things first.

'What Johanna?' she says, her head all tipped to one side.

'Fanny!' I shove the dead dolly in her face then run away. She screams and runs after me. I run round and round the back green with our dead dolly in my hand then I throw it at her and run upstairs.

'Well, the beater was broken,' is all mother says but Jemima cries her heart out. That night when our father comes home her bottom lip is still wobbling so he makes her another one. But it's not the same. Not for me.

Jemima hugs the new wooden spoon dolly and calls it Fanny again but I don't call it Victoria. Playing's finished for me.

***

With every mile that set Haddington behind us my heart grew lighter. I would manage. I was a manager – I would cope. I would go back to mother and bring the children up in Gordon Street, the very place I was brought up. The bus jiggled me up and down, up and down, Leith coming closer, and closer.

Mother's hands are red raw with scrubbing at the washboard. She's got a big board and a wee one. The wee one, for hankies, flannels and socks, is mine. After a morning washing hankies my fingers go white and shrivelled up like prunes. I am a worker now.

I listen to the women that come in to the house; the aunts and half-sisters, neighbours and friends. At first it's noise and laughter or moans, then it's stories and words I understand. They moan about work, then they moan about men, all the time their hands stringing beans or darning socks.

'Half they layabouts in Leith have nae work,' mother says, 'they stand aboot the streets wi their hands in their pockets.'

'Aye, an dae they lift their hands to turn a mangle?' says another.

'Or chop a neep?'

'Whit? Men? Ha! Lift a jar mair like.'

Till I'm shaking my head the way they do, and laughing when they do.

'Aye, work. It'll be the death o' us,' they all chorus. You're cursed both ways – cursed if ye have work, cursed if ye don't.

***

The bus pulled up at our stop. Then I saw it; Gordon Street and the door to our stair. I struggled up the worn stone steps, my kist hitting my knee and the children hushed now. Wee Jane banged her fist at the front door. Of course, the door wasn't locked. I could have turned the knob and walked in. But I had taught the bairns to knock. So we waited. If I expected a handshake, or even a welcome smile, I was let down. 'Johanna,' mother said, her face drawn, not even fully opening the door.

'I made a terrible mistake mother,' I blurted out. 'I can't stay with him. He's a drinker, I mean a bad drinker and he's an auld man. He lied to me. He's no guid to us mither. I've left him.' The children dived under her long skirt and ran into the house. 'I've come home,' I said, pushing the door, then she had to let me in. I wasn't two steps over that threshold and I cried for my terrible mistake, the familiar wrapping about me. The bairns ran through the house, jumping up and down and cheering. This was a holiday for them. And their cousins were here. Gladys, my half-sister, was back living in Gordon Street. I wiped my face and glanced out of the familiar window. Down on the street there were still bairns skipping and playing the old street games. I wanted that for my bairns. I wanted them to jump peevers and learn all the street songs I knew. And Jane could go to Flora Stevenson's school and who knows but she might be a teacher one day.

Mother made me tea, her face drawn and worn looking. Gladys was busy fussing over the bairns. The well-known smells came back to me; the stewed tea and the tripe and onions boiling in a cast iron pan. Jane Scott drained her tea, set her cup on the table, snatched in a long breath through her tight lips then looked hard at me. 'Ye've made yer bed Johann – lie in it!'

I am lingering to look in a shop window.

I hate working in the shoe shop. I am fourteen and want to see the world. I want to make something of myself. And I'm in no hurry to go home. And there's father, on his way home from work when he spots me. He thinks I'm admiring my reflection in the window. There's a right black mood on him and no doubt the hankering after a drink. Next thing I know he's grabbing me by the arm and pushing me down the street, shouting, 'shame on ye hussie! Shame on ye!'

'Och, leave the lassie alone,' mother says, after he pushed me up the stairs and bundled me into the house, 'she's doubtless dreamin' o' the man she'll marry and let's hope he's a better man than you Tam Blackie.' But I am not dreaming of who I'll marry. Marriage, if ever it is to come, seems a long way off. I want to leave home. I want to do something real. Something good.

I might be fourteen but I still want to play. Still want to get back early from the shoe shop and skip with the other girls in the street;

My love's a soldier
In lands far away
A true-hearted laddie
Sae gallant and gay.

And though we all sing about love it's just a song. None of the lassies in the street has a soldier love in lands far away – but we all sing as though we do. That song runs through my mind now, maybe to numb the harsh words bouncing back and forth across the kitchen. I rub my arm where father squeezed it.

'Ye pickled herring,' mother shouts at him. 'Soused! Look at ye? Wi' a nose on ye like a bramble.'

'Huv ye hud a keek at yersel wumin? Ye're no the Pretty Polly you used tae be.'

I press my hands up to my ears and close my eyes. The last time my half-brother Jimmie took me to Portobello we went into the magic hall of mirrors and I saw my reflection all bumpy and wavy. Like a ghost from the grave. What a laugh. And we had tea in a tea room and Jimmie said it tasted like it had been stewing for a week. He said his tea spoon could stand up in it. He said, why don't you have a go at reading the tea leaves wee sister, and I shook my head and said no.

Mother is at the tea pot pouring tea. 'And wit's wrong wi a bit o' vanity anyhow?' she says. Father sits at the table now, holding his cup with his calloused hands. 'Wha's it going tae hurt?' she says, splashing milk into his tea. 'She's hardly going off tae marry a Prince – being a Blackie – so let the lassie be. Man, wit's the matter wi' a wee bit dream? Christ Almighty, there's no much else is there?'

Jumping over the waves – that is great fun. And if you get your bloomers wet they soon dry out.

Mother bangs a cup of tea down on the table for me. I sit down between them and drink it. We all slurp our tea and don't talk. Children don't talk to adults and women don't talk much to men. Father sighs and drains his cup and there we sit, silence, disappointment and poverty wrapping its thin grey shawl about us.

'The lassie doesnae like the shoe shop,' mother says suddenly, getting up and stamping over to the cupboard where she keeps her beer. My grip tightens around my cup. This isn't a good time to tell him.

'Well, she can thole it.'

***

Mother said it again, slower this time. 'Ye made yer bed. Now lie in it.' My jaw fell open. Tears rolled down my face. She didn't understand. I shook my head. I tugged at her sleeve. 'But he's threatened to kill me mother. He's threatened us with a knife. And he's a drinker. And auld. He lied to me. He's an auld man. A drunk auld man. I made a terrible mistake. Mother, I'm scared for the bairns.'

'I've no room.'

'He's a drunkard. And he…'

'Lie in it lassie. Lie in it.'

I couldn't believe it. How could she? Was there no ounce of feeling in the woman? I stood up and staggered backwards, feeling drunk myself. I felt as though she had punched me in the stomach. Gladys had gone quiet and even the bairns stopped their racket. Without saying another word I gathered up Jane, Mina and Jamesy, lifted my kist and left the house as quickly as I could. Mother stayed sitting at the table, looking down. Not even a cheerio was uttered between us. Gladys came to the door and waved as I hurried down the dim stairwell, the bairns bawling now because they'd just arrived on their holidays and here was I, cruel mother, whisking them away.

We took the bus back to Haddington – where the bad bed I had made lay waiting for me. The wheels trundled. The horse clomped slowly. The journey took forever. Yellow rape fields and dark people blurred past. Dogs barked at the bus. The children fell asleep. My chin fell to my chest.

The sermon in the church is about the War.

Everything is about the war. And how important it is to keep the home fires burning. There's already rumours that Grange house is to be commandeered, and how we should start to apply for other positions. I'm told I'll get a fine reference. Or I could go into the factories, they tell me. At nineteen there's no end to the work I could do. But I want to stay here. I pick up my skirts and run out of the church. They've hardly finished the last hymn. I shove one hand over my hat to keep it in place. Grace has come out after me. She's calling 'Johanna.' I don't heed her. She knows where I'm going and warned me against it. She might not be the marrying sort, but she isn't me. Swallows swoop low, like they're teasing me. I cut through the field of barley and grains fly up. I tear at stalks. I feel like a child again. 'Johanna,' Grace calls, 'come back.'

I hasten on, over the fields and down the grassy bank to the river. I feel feathery and glad. I can see a few boats on the river. I am all in a tangle, my hair has come loose and spilled down my back. The hem of my Sunday skirt has caught grass stalks and a bright head of pimpernel. I'm panting fast. I can't see him. Perhaps he is out in his boat? I stand on the bank and peer up and down the river. My throat tightens. Where is he? Where is James Melville?

'A boat, madam?'

I gasp and swing round.

'Careful now, you don't want to fall in.' But it isn't James. It's a much older man.

I blurt out, 'the oarsman…James Melville…I…I..'

'It's only us old ones left,' the man says and shrugs, looking awkward, as if he is apologising for his age. His eyes are pools of pain.

'But…I don't understand.'

'The war miss. The bloody war. Kitchener issued a call…'

I lift my skirts and run. Away from the river. Away from the old man. Away from the bloody war. Grace is still there beyond the field. She is still calling for me. I shout her name and there she is, running into the barley field to meet me. I fall into her arms and let the tears come then.

'They've all gone, Johanna,' she says, 'all the young men have gone.'

***

Jane woke up and smiled at me. As the bus trundled along the coast road she kept asking where we were going now. I pointed out the villages of Tranent then the bonny little village of Pencaitland. Jamesy was asleep in my arms. Mina had woken and was pressing her nose against the window pane. I took Jane up on my knee. Though she was too young to understand she was the only one I could speak to. 'I've just got to go back and take a' the bairns God gives me,' I told her. She nodded, as though she understood.

'Aye mammy,' the wee lassie said, 'that's right.'

I was back before Willie was home. When he came in that evening I said nothing about my flight. The only difference that day was that we had pies bought from the butcher instead of a proper cooked meal. Willie looked at me strangely, maybe guessing the journey I'd taken. He ate in silence. After tea he told Jane one of his ghost stories. I waited for him to lift his bowler hat from the peg and go out but he didn't. I went about my duties, washing the dishes while he frightened the bairns to death.

'Did ye hear about thon mannie used to walk the streets after midnight and howl like a wolf?' Willie was calling to me.

I turned from my dishes, my hands dripping wet. 'No faither. I never heard that one.'

'Oh aye – and if young lassies had stayed out late they could bump into him. One lassie lived to tell the tale. She met him in a dark alley and said how he sprouted hairs on his face and howled at her and when she looked down inside his mouth she saw fangs and a pool o' blood.'

'Heavens!'

'Aye, and then he sprang on her, wanting to sink these great long fangs into her white neck but she was strong for a lassie and pushed him off – even though he was strong as an ox. Turned out she wasn't a lassie at all but a she-devil, strong as seven men and she had been walking the dark streets looking for a soul to take possession o'. They were as wicked as each other.'

'Faither –the bairns. Ye'll gie them nightmares.'

'Nonsense – nothing like a guid story, eh bairns. Well, this she-devil got hold o' this werewolf and hurled him into a sewer and that's why they stink to this day.'

'Who stinks?' asked wee Jane.

'The sewers,' answered Willie, grinning. Then he sat back and lit his pipe and still I was waiting for him to go out, like the vampire of his tale, and prowl the dark streets in search of whisky and beer, and a mournful tune crooned in some cobbled alley. But he looked over to where I was standing, framed in the kitchen doorway, and gave me his old rogue smile.

I sighed and shook my head. 'Willie. Oh Willie,' I said, going back to my drying dishes.

He got up and put a hand on my shoulder, brushed my hair back and planted a wet kiss on my cheek. 'Yer lookin bonny tonight, Mrs Lockhart.'

10

The following year Donald was born. Four children in four years and us still in that small room and kitchen. We were poor right enough, on account of faither's drinking but these bairns were as well dressed as any. Every stitch on them was made by me. I'd got into the habit of visiting the church jumble sales, at the end just before they started packing up. There I could buy a dozen old jumpers for a penny, unravel the wool at home and make brand new jumpers and cardigans. The bairns bellies were always filled and every day I thanked my ten years in domestic service for preparing me for this.

Mrs Baxter had taken to visiting, even though it was a long bus journey.

'But it gi'es me something to do, Johanna,' she said, grinning and tickling the bairns. For it was true, she was let go of. 'And good riddance to them,' she said, 'and knock-knock?' she said.

'Who's there?' Jane and Mina screamed. They loved old Mrs Baxter and her jokes.

'Isabel,' she said.

'Isabel who?' shouted the girls.

'Isabel necessary on a bike?' Then she would hoot with laughter and the girls would too though I don't think they knew much about bikes and bells. But it was good to laugh. And to snatch bits of talk about James Melville. Baxter loved hearing about James Melville.

'If ever I loved,' she said with a sigh, 'it would be to someone as gallant as your hero, James Melville.'

'You never saw anyone as strong as he,' I said, when the children were out the back playing.

'Better to have loved for a short while, than never,' she said, wiping a tear from her eye. 'Tell me again, Johanna, about that time he took you out on the river.'

I was glad to tell her and no doubt the tale grew with each telling. His hair grew darker, his muscles stronger, the sun on the river brighter. Our precious few times together stretched as long as the river Tay.

I always felt perked up after a visit from old Mrs Baxter. 'I would take ye if I could,' she said, 'but there's barely the place for me as it is.' Baxter had moved in with her sister in her one room and kitchen and slept in the kitchen where her bed was a shake down in front of the fire. 'And anyway,' she said with a wink, 'who knows but handsome Mr Melville may yet turn up and whisk ye off.'

'Chance would be a fine thing,' I said, laughing with her, but it was that very hope kept me going. Every time she visited Baxter fanned my hopes with her stories of soldiers, taken for dead, turning up on doorsteps.

My womb had two years break, and that because I was learning how to keep Willie's clawing hands off me; plying him with malted milk then turning away, feigning sleep. When Donald was two Thomas was born. Five bairns under seven plus us two in a pokey room and kitchen. Grey hairs in my head, lines about my eyes and mouth, and me little more than thirty.

I gazed into the mirror, my face a map of suffering and determination, wondering how on earth we were going to survive. Willie's pay packet shrunk month by month. I lifted a lock of hair and squinted at the white thread-mark on my forehead. I peered closer. It was growing, I was sure it was, like a river bursting its banks. I shook down my hair and set my jaw for the mirror, willing the glass not to crack. The first seven years of married life had been hard enough. Pray God the next seven would bring us luck.

Mirror, mirror on the wall.

I gaze into father's cracked mirror, the glass he squints into when he's trimming his beard. I picture myself in a pretty cap. A parlour maid, perhaps? Or maybe I could be a cook? In a fine house, spick and span and nobody drunk there, nobody falling over. Half the girls in Edinburgh and Leith go into service. It will give me a chance to get away – see something of the world. Father has his strong opinions about kow-towing to the toffs and how no Blackie will ever stoop to that. But when I see the maids and cooks and house-keepers and butlers off on errands in the shops or haggling with the fish-wives on street corners to buy fish for the Friday dinner I admire them. They always look smart and clean. They always look important. They look as though a house will fall to its knees if not for them and their hard work. Nobody falls down drunk in fine houses. I stare at my young face with that imaginary white bonnet over my black hair. Yes ma'am, I imagine myself saying, softly, properly. Certainly ma'am.

***

It was the first warm day of spring. I opened the kitchen window to fling out a scrap of bacon rind. Sweet warm air wafted in. Above the houses the green Garleton hill sloped and called. Noises from the street caught me; the rumble of cart wheels, a cry of a woman, a stone skited. Wings beat. Above me a gull screamed and swooped to grab the rind. The gull took off with its prize but I stayed at the open window, breathing. I gulped in air as if I was drowning. The bairns cried at my back. Even two snatched minutes to myself and they wanted me with them. For once I let them cry. I felt Donald cling to my leg. I felt the thick cotton of my stocking slip. I heard the snap of the button. I let the stocking rumple down. I had to keep looking at the hills, and breathing. God knows it hadn't been warm for months. It was still early, so the chimney fires hadn't dirtied the air yet. I noticed how sun rays fell on gold patches of hillside. I felt as though, if my arm was long enough, I could reach out and catch that light.

We could have a picnic? Grace was always saying there was nothing like fresh air. We could have a day's holiday, bask a bit in the first sunlight of the year, why not? I had a hundred reasons why not, cleaning the house and buying and cooking his dinner among them, but in that moment no reason was strong enough. I swung round, decided. 'Bairns,' I declared, 'we're going on a picnic!'

I fiddled with my stocking and re-buttoned it. Only Jane seemed to know what a picnic was. Her face lit up like the sun. Seeing the joy on her face was reason enough. 'A real picnic?' she cried, like I was offering her a crock of gold.

'A proper picnic,' I replied, clapping my hands. I hurried to get ready. I found the basket, took the tea towels out of it bar one. That would serve us as a table-cloth. I boiled eggs and cut slices of bread. I wrapped salt in a twist of newspaper and sent Jane out to the stand pipe to fill two bottles of water.

By this time the children were jumping up and down. 'Picnic, picnic, we're going on a picnic,' Jane sang and the others joined in. I hurried a comb through their hair then tugged it through my own. The clock snapped the precious seconds. It was twenty five minutes to ten. Willie wouldn't be home till twelve. 'Aye,' I said to the bairns, 'we've plenty time for a picnic.'

There were two dirty nappies that needed cleaning, and that morning the eggs took forever. It was nearer ten when we were finally ready. I bundled us all out the door. 'We're off to the hills,' I said, sang more like, giving Jane the basket. Mina carried the water bottles. Jamesy grabbed hold of my skirt. I carried Donald in one arm and wee Gordon in the other. What a relief to be out. Jane stomped ahead then stopped and swung round. 'But…mother…where are the hills?'

'Not far,' I said.

'So which way do we go?' she asked me.

Just go. I wanted to say. It's spring. Who knows but I might bump into

James Melville. I don't think he died after all. Stop asking questions. I don't know which way. 'The end of the street,' I said, 'then we'll see the hills.' I walked faster. Wee Jamesy couldn't keep up. I couldn't carry three.

There was a crowd outside the bakers shop. I think it was the smell they liked for there often was a crowd gathered there. I wove through a huddle of women. 'You dinnae ken how tae say no, dae ye?' someone muttered. I felt tears smart my eyes. Jamesy fell and cried out. Someone in the crowd picked him up and brushed him down. I whisked him up and put him into Jane's arms. Mina carried the basket and the bottles. 'Keep going bairns,' I said, hurrying along the street, my heart racing with the shame. 'We'll get our picnic soon.' Nothing was going to spoil this outing. Nothing! I sang as I marched,

Bonnie wee thing, canty wee thing,
lovely wee thing, wert thou mine,
I would wear thee in my bosom,
lest my jewel I should tine.

Me and Jemima get to stand on the pavement on Saturday afternoons to wait for the bear.

One-eyed Mr Moody walks past every Saturday in the summertime, him and his great lumbering bear on a chain. People say Mr Moody lost his eye because that bear with his ferocious claws swiped him one. I don't know if that's true because Mr Moody never seems scared of his bear and the bear doesn't look ferocious. The bear walks on two legs. At first I think it's a big man in a fur coat, till I see he's got claws on his fingers and he's got a snout. When they walk right past us I can smell it is a real bear.

'Roll up, roll up, peen tae see the show,' shouts Mr Moody. 'Harry the hairy bear. Right here. Scotland's finest and wildest and ladies and gentlemen, girls and boys, maist right fearsome, performing bear.' We don't have a peen. It's enough to see the bear plod past, slow and heavy and sad. We never get to see the real show – but the bairns that go say the bear crushes apples in his hand and peels bananas then eats them in one go, then kicks a ball then gets up on a wobbly chair and they say they all laugh till their sides ache.

So the bear joins the rest of them, dancing in the shadows on the wall when the candles and the gas lamps are lit at night and the flames from the coal fire leap in the grate. I am scared of Coconut Tam but I feel sorry for the bear. He's got the saddest eyes I have ever seen and sometimes, lying in bed thinking about the bear and how people laugh at him trying to balance on a wobbly chair, I greet.

***

It felt forever we strode along Haddington High Street. 'Up this next lane,' I shouted ahead to Jane, who was leading with wee Gordon in her arms.

'Will the sunny hill be up the lane?' she called back.

But I never did answer her. We turned the corner and there he was; Willie Lockhart. 'Just where dae ye think ye're galavantin tae?' he said.

'I might ask you the same question,' I said, my eyes taking in the glass of beer and the red glow on his face. It was barely half past ten in the morning. What was Willie Lockhart doing leaning on the door of the public house at half past ten in the morning? 'For God's sake man,' I hissed. I clutched the bairns tight.

'Johann!'

Mother's voice. Sometimes so hard it cuts through me like a knife. 'Stand ootside the pub and shout fir yer faither tae come hame.' That used to be Jemima's job. Now it's my turn.

I stand at the open door of the public house. The air inside is blue with cigarette smoke, the place a blur with men's voices and cloth caps and spitting. My wee voice is lost in their loud laughing and curses. 'My faither's tae come home,' I call at the open door, but no-one inside pays any heed. I'm not the only five year old lassie standing miserably at the door of the public house.

***

'We're going to the hills,' Jane told him, 'for a picnic!'

He laughed. 'Oh aye, the hills? And wha's going to mak my dinner?' He raised the glass that was in his hand. Beads of brown liquid ran down the side. In the dark smoky public house at his back a man was calling for him to play his hand in dominoes.

'Wha's that?' the man shouted from inside. 'Wha're ye talking tae?'

'My wee wifie,' Willie said, 'aff fir a picnic!'

'Noo, which wee wifie wid that be?' I heard one of his cronies call out with a cackle. I was appalled with the lot of them

I swung round, disgusted. 'Come on bairns,' I said. 'This is no place fir bairns.' Then I glared at Willie Lockhart. 'And no place fir you either.'

Willie tried to ruffle Jane's hair but she scowled at him. Wee Jamesy came forward and punched him on the leg. Willie laughed a hollow sounding laugh. 'Mither,' he says, puffing out his chest. 'I hae jist cause to celebrate. And so do you. Bairns,' he shouted, lifting his glass into the air so the sunlight slanted through the brown beer. 'We're going tae a grand hill. Arthur's Seat. Your guid faither here is having himself a wee drink to celebrate. We're leaving Haddington and no before time. We're going tae Edinburgh! Yer faither here has got himself a new job,' and he flung an arm out to the side like a music hall star. 'And no jist any job. Oh no!'

'What's wrong with the job you've got? What's happened to the shop?' I could feel a blind panic rise through me.

'Woman, hud on and let a man tell his story. Edinburgh, fine capital o' Scotland, is a grand toon wi' mony a man with a watch.'

'Aye?' I said, rocking the bairns so hard they started to cry. 'And?'

'And – in that grand town there is a fancy shop called Brooks.' Although he was a short man he swelled up and looked at least six feet. He said Brooks as though it was Buckingham palace. 'And the man you are now staring at has landed a job there. It's our lucky day. We'll be made. Great wages and new clothes for everybody.'

'What happened to your shop faither?' I said, slowly, spelling out, spitting out, every word. I could tell he wanted to slap me one. Here he was, all blown up by his news, having a drink or five 'tae celebrate' and here was I, tearing him down to size. He flashed his eyes at me and glowered.

'Wheesht mother and keep your nose to your own business. Away hame, pack the kist and good riddance to this dump.'

Then he turned round and strutted back into the public house, a few inches smaller. I'd taken him down a peg and he hated me for it. I stood at the door of the public house and shouted in, 'I've heard what they've been saying about ye Willie Lockhart. I've seen the unpaid bills. You're a drunkard. That's what ye are – a drunkard!' The bairns were all crying by now. I didn't care. Let them see what kind of a father they had. 'Your wee shop had to close, didn't it? You're up to your ears in debt, admit it Willie. Here ye are, spending money on drink, and what are yer poor bairns eating, eh? Tell me that! Tell me…'

He slammed the door in my face.

The hills and their sunlight had gone out of me. I backed away from the door, reeling. I thought I would fall down. More than him and his new job I couldn't believe I'd come to be the sort of woman that stands at the door of the public house and shouts, putting the dirty laundry on display and deliberately trying to shame her husband. I clamped my hand over my mouth. What was wrong with me? I wanted to throw up. I breathed deeply, trying desperately to still this spinning top that was my life.

Jane slipped her hand in mine. 'Faither's got a new job,' she said, and smiled up at me.

I sighed and nodded. 'Aye, yer faither's got a new job.' The bairns stopped crying. We walked home. Maybe, just maybe, everything would be fine in Edinburgh.

That night, when the bairns were asleep and Willie not yet home I sat drumming my fingers on the table. Then I ran to the door and checked Willie was not staggering along the street. There was no sign of him. I hurried to write a letter. If I didn't I would burst, or sink to my knees and weep.

76 Cobbler's Wynd
Haddington
23rd September 1929

My dearest James

Just thinking of you makes my heart strong again. Oh, James I am tested sorely. He is a drinker. I am afraid he will find these letters. I have caught him rummaging in my boxes for coins for beer. I, who uphold honesty, have grown secretive.

Until I learn where you are I will send your letters to Mrs Baxter. She was the cook in Trinity. Sometimes she visits me, with her jokes that lifts my spirits. She says if we didn't laugh we would surely weep. She has promised not to open the letters and she has little time for Willie and his ways. He had the cheek to call her old! That set her against him, if she wasn't before. That's the kettle calling the pot black, for if anyone is old it's him. But enough of him. Oh yes, enough of him. He is having us flitting soon.

These pages are a place I go to meet you. My ink is our river. My words are the meadows and fields and hills at Comrie. I pray one day you may go to the university and read fine books. This war has turned the dreams of young men into ash.

But this I pray for you, that you are one of the forgetful ones, not the dead. That you are one of the men wandering the byways of France and that people care for you and nurse you back to health. And birds sing for you. Sun shines for you. The horrors in your mind subside and flowers grow for you. The bairns at least are a comfort to me. As are you. May God preserve you.

Johanna xxx

I can't thole the sight of my own faither drinking, seeing him reeling about the room like a fool and him thinking he's so funny and that everybody has to laugh and clap and cheer when he punches the air and falls down on the bed, squashing me and Jemima.

'Playing time's done Johann –and that fancy learnin's a' done wi' – wit's wrang? No like the real world? Feart o' real work, is that it?'

'I'm a good worker faither.' I watch him try to stand up then fall back into his chair.

'Guid worker's thole it. Think I like walkin a' the way tae Liberton every day? Think I'd no rather lie in ma bed? Well listen tae me lassie – I thole it –and wit fir? Wit dae I work fir? Fir ye. Yir mither got ye that job an it's no every lassie can get a job in a shop – and a shoe shop tae boot.' He laughed at the joke, once he realised he had made it.

'Yir faither's talking sense, Johann,' says mother and she's pouring beer from a brown bottle into a chipped cup and I want to smash that cup and I want to run out of that house and I want to keep running until all my crying is done and I'm in some better place than this.

'You young ones have no idea,' he says, holding on to the table's edge, swaying like he's on a boat. 'School till fourteen? Nae bloody idea wit real work is. And noo- coz ye dinnae like the smell – poor wee sowel – you think ye can just walk oot and leave it. D'ye think I like the niff o' dung and rotten compost and blighted tatties? Wit do I trap rabbits for? So you can eat, that's what! D'ye think I'm ower fond o howking neeps in the cold an' the rain and the howling wind? Oh, my nose, ma poor wee nose. Help me somebody, I canny stand the smell!'

He falls back onto the seat and mother puts the bottle of beer on the table in front of him. That's when I push my chair back and get up. I lunge over and swipe out at the half bottle of beer on the table and send it flying. I watch a spout of brown frothy liquid shoot up in the air. It gushes, but leisurely, like everything has slowed down. It's like a peaty waterfall, with white foam. It's beautiful. It's reaching, reaching, like it's breaking free, then curves and falls, soaking him. I turn on my heels and run out that house and down the stairs, three at a time. I hear him shouting and swearing. I grab my skirt and jump down six steps at a time.

My heart is pounding when I push open the stair door and fall out onto Gordon Street. It's dark and the gas lamps drop sickly yellow patches along the pavement. I run, avoiding the lit patches, like a fugitive, and make for Constitution Street. I don't know where I'm going. I just have to get away. The street is busy, with men mostly, coming back from the late shift at the docks. I run down towards the Docks. I want to see ships and water. I want to get as far away as I can. I dodge the men on the streets and some of them push me. I am hardly ever out this late. I'm frightened. I run past public houses, through bands of hot fuggy air where laughter and hard voices hit the night air as I pass.

Out of the dark shadows I see someone come towards me. 'Come here you,' a gruff voice calls, and I turn and run back the way I came, my heart hammering. I'm petrified. The streets are a dark dangerous forest and I'm in it lost and alone. I can run fast. I glance back and there's nobody there. Blindly I run on, tears streaming down my face. I hate being out alone so late but I can't go back to the house. Father will kill me.

My half-sister Martha lives half a mile away in Jane Street. She knows what father's like. And Martha is always good to me. I speed up Leith Walk towards Jane Street.

The relief of being inside by the warm cosy fire is immense. Martha makes me tea and gives me the seat beside the fire. I wake the baby up with my gasping and panting and crying and talking.

'Go into service, Johanna,' Martha says, patting my trembling arm. I nod and grasp at her hand. 'I would if I was you. It'll suit you to a T.'

11

I wrapped the plates and cups in newspaper and placed them carefully down into the kist. I'd heard of Brooks. Maybe this was our lucky break? It was 1929. There were many men with no work and I was lucky my man had a job. And not just any job, I told myself like I'd told myself a hundred times. Willie Lockhart was a watchmaker. And Edinburgh was a grand place was it not? The capital of Scotland. With a capital C.

I took the cutlery from the drawer and wrapped the forks, spoons and knives in dish cloths. The house was quiet now. The only sounds, the bairns soft snores in their beds and the dull tread of my feet on the floor boards. As I pressed rolls of spoons and ladles into the kist I was pressing away parts of myself; the self that had wanted it all to be so different from how it was; that young Johanna in the photograph, her that had dared to dream of a fine handsome loving man. James Melville sailed into my mind. I squeezed my fist into the kist, over the cutlery wrapped in tea towels, and laughed an emptied-out laugh.

Gordon Street was slum in the Lockhart's eyes and I was weak in trying to defend it. And ever since I'd gone 'running hame tae mammy' as Willie called it because word got to him after all, I'd been forced to hold my tongue. 'Yer mammy who didn't want ye,' he went on. On and on when he was drunk. And what could I say? He was right.

Would Edinburgh make it any better? I sat down at the kitchen table, picked up the last tea cup and turned it round in my hands. I sighed so long my ribs hurt. Not just my ribs. My heart hurt. The real thoughts; the ones I'd been pushing into the dark, rose up and I was back there. Young again.

In the dining hall I lower my eyes if any male servant asks me to pass the salt or the pepper and when I go to bed I bolt the door and Lizzie says it's probably no bad thing.

Mostly though, when I go to bed, Lizzie is already asleep. Night after night I climb the stone steps to our room in the attic and hobble into the dark room. I light the candle. 'Goodness, my feet are killing me,' I whisper, partly to check whether Lizzie is awake or not. Then I gaze at my reflection in the mirror. Perhaps it's the candle's soft glow but it seems to me that the face staring back looks almost beautiful.

Lizzie isn't asleep. I hear her stir in her bed. 'It's these errands you run Johanna,' she says, 'above everything else it's too much.'

I pull off my mutch cap, lay it on the table and shake out my hair. I untie my boots and ease my feet out of them. 'Ah! Now that's better. It's my feet Lizzie. They're growing too fast. That's the trouble. And I don't like to ask for new boots again.'

'But you must, Johanna. You'll be a cripple if you don't.' Lizzie sighs then yawns. We speak in such whispers even the mice won't hear us.

'I'm sorry,' I whisper, 'to be waking you up. Me and Grace were chatting downstairs. How time flies when it's our own time, eh? I'll blow this out in a minute.' I lift the brush to begin my nightly one hundred brushes. By twenty I can hear the small puttering snores of Lizzie. Good. With Lizzie asleep I can imagine the small attic room is my own. And I don't want to blow the candle out. I want to gaze into the mirror brushing my thick black hair until the moon steals into the room. Until the room is a river and I am being rowed down that river.

***

I wrapped the last cup in newspaper and set it down in the kist. God knows, I had hoped for more. I, Johanna Blackie, had fondly imagined I'd sail up the glorious golden river of Leith Walk, board a train and journey to a better world. And in that world I had dared to imagine a pure, gallant kind of love. I imagined it would be a good man, like Mr James Melville, that would take my hand. But I married Willie Lockhart. Now here I was, stacking my life into my kist and it wasn't just my life any more. I had five bairns, a drunkard for a husband and we were off. Off to board in two rooms in a lodging house with two bachelors. Edinburgh! It'll all be fine in Edinburgh, mother. Just you wait till we're in Edinburgh. Because Mr Lockhart here has got himself a fine job in Edinburgh.

I got up and wrapped the knives in a bundle. My heart kicked at the sudden noise of a man shouting outside on the street. It was dark outside. I heard a door bang. But the noise passed. It wasn't my door that banged. It wasn't my man. It was some other drunk returning home. I looked up at the clock on the wall. It was ten o'clock already. I braced myself against his return.

I carried on packing, my jaw set hard against my lot. The gas mantle flickered and hissed. Pressing small things now, like combs and ribbons into the corners, I breathed deeply. 'Help me God,' I whispered, 'and make me strong.' For the bairns I wanted to do my best. I pressed my hands together and watched the gas flame turn blue then putter and die out. But I wouldn't die. Resolve pounded inside me like a drum. I could feel my whole body charge as though I'd been filled up by a lightning bolt. Aye, whatever life and poverty and this marriage slung at me – I would survive, and so would the bairns. More than survive, God willing, they would thrive. I would make the best of this bed I had made.

I went to bed that night with a stirring sense that something had changed in me. Willie staggered in true to form, tripping in the dark and stinking of whisky and wanting his way with me. 'Wheesht now man,' I said, an edge to my words that sounded new, strong, 'leave us all in peace and just wheesht. Ye frightened the bairns enough the day. Wheesht.' I showed him my back and wrapped the hard woollen blanket about me. He didn't pester me further. Soon the drunkard was loud in his world of dreams and I was in mine.

And God help me but it was always the same. Always the handsome boatman. In life we'd only met a handful of times, but eleven years had passed since then, and I swear in those years I'd met him a thousand times.

What Willie by my side dreamt, I don't know. A world where the working man holds his head high and the aristocracy are run out of town, them and their velvet coats and snooty voices gone the way of the French. A world of freedom, equality and communism. Or perhaps it's a good malt whisky he dreamt of, and a mournful tune on the fiddle. Or for all I knew of him perhaps it was another woman he dreamt of, one softer than I and one happy to nestle into his arms. A river grew between us, flowing fast with beer and whisky and tears, getting wider and wider.

I wondered if I could swim back, up the river, and start again. Make wiser choices. I heard Gordon cry out in his sleep. I heard Donald cough. I heard Jane talk in her sleep. *A peen to see the puppet show,* she murmured.

I tried to sleep. *A peen to see him cry*, I'd need plenty strength the next day for the flitting. I pressed my eyes tight shut. *A peen to see the auld man, auld man, auld man…*

The kist was packed.

Sitting in the sky.

12

We're to lodge in a two-roomed house in Montague Street in Newington, Edinburgh. Mon-tae-gay, he calls it. And we're to share the house with two bachelors. And we'll have a grand old time with the wages I'll be bringing home, just you wait, says he. Aye, and I'll wait, says me. Though I didn't trust him as far as I could throw him, hope, as Grace liked to quote, springs eternal. It must after the blows and shame I'd suffered for here was I, butterflies doing a merry jig in my breast. Edinburgh! Not Leith. Not Haddington, but the capital city herself. 'It'll be grand, mother, just you wait.'

I was that happy to be leaving Haddington and all the gossips behind I flung my arms around his craggy neck. 'I hope so faither. Edinburgh's a lovely place.'

'Aye, it's none of your Leith neither. This is Edinburgh proper. Now, what do you fancy for when you go out walking in that bonny city – a fancy new dress or a good warm coat?'

I was fool enough to put my finger to my lips, tip my head, close my eyes and say, 'now, let me think. Oh, I can't choose faither. I just can't choose between them. You choose.'

'Well, I tell you what Mrs Lockhart. Have both!'

I'm in service a few months when I meet up with Sadie Macdonald in the church.

She's sitting with the other servants from Cuthie Bank House and in the middle of a rousing 'all things bright and beautiful' Sadie notices me, flashes a wide grin, stops singing and waves. I don't dare wave back. We seem all too proper in Grange House to do that, but I smile and after church Sadie and I shake hands like long lost friends.

Work all week long is no burden, especially knowing, come Sunday, me and Sadie will dander around Comrie arm in arm, both of us talking twenty to the dozen.

'I swear Johanna, the gardener has taken a fancy to me.'

'Don't heed him Sadie. Lower your eyes and look down.'

'And him that delivers the groceries, he winked at me.'

'Never heed him neither Sadie. Heed none o' them.'

'But what about you, Johanna? Is there no stable lad or boot boy that turns your bonny head?'

I shake my bonny head. 'He'd have to be finer than a stable lad, and finer than a boot boy,' I say and I'm filled with this sudden image of me in a white silk gown and kid gloves and a proper gent walking towards me through long grass.

I hardly hear Sadie. She tugs at my sleeve and laughs. 'We're servant girls, you and me.' The image fades and I'm staring down at Sadie's open palms, like I am a fortune teller. 'My poor young hands Johanna,' she cries. 'Red from a' that laundry. And chapped. It's the borax. Look at them. How can a girl get married wi' chapped hands like that?' Sadie's pretty face looks ready to crumple.

'What you need is a sheep,' I say and pull Sadie in the direction of a field of sheep. 'Lizzie told me. You plunge yer hands into their wool – if you can get hold o' one, then all the chapped skin vanishes. It's the lanolin. It's a wonder for the skin.'

But we never do manage to catch one – so I don't know if Lizzie was havering or not. But we have great fun running about that field – like a couple of collie dogs – wi our Sunday clothes on too!

***

We arrived at a street of dark high tenement buildings, smoke belching from a hundred coal fires. We stood on the street and looked up, giddy after the long journey. I'd forgotten how high tenements were, how black the stone from all the smoke. I'd forgotten how busy the streets were, and noisy. Arthur's Seat with its crags and mountains loomed behind, looking like some highland scenery had lost its way and fallen down at the edge of Montague Street.

'Here we are then mither,' Willie said when we had hoisted our belongings up the dim stairwell and stood before the door. The bairns couldn't stand still they were that excited. A shaft of light spilled in from the window at the top of the stairwell. The door was painted olive green. Drab I thought, wishing it was bright yellow. At the side of the door there was a brass bell pull. Willie pulled it and while it clanged away I put up a quick prayer.

'Mother, mother, is this our new home? Is this Edinburgh?' Donald said, patting the door.

'Aye son, but take your hand off the door.' Too late. The door swung open and wee Donald fell head first into the hallway. The landlady shrieked and jumped back.

'Sorry, oh, I'm very sorry,' I blurted out, blushing, shaking my head and hauling Donald to his feet again. What a start. 'He's that excited. Sorry ma'am.'

'Should think so too,' said the woman, brushing herself down, then ushering us into the house. 'Didn't think you had so many bairns.' She watched us troop in, her head nodding as she counted. My heart sank. What lie had Willie told her? 'Anyway, you'd better come away in. You'll be tired,' she said, putting a brighter face on the business of welcoming us into our new home.

We weren't alone in the two-roomed house. The two bachelors were already well installed. 'Mr Pearson and Mr Walls,' said our landlady, nodding to the next room. I imagined two gentlemen in brown suits sitting peacefully in their room, drinking tea, reading books and keeping civil tongues in their heads.

I put the kist down on the wooden floor. It had grown heavier over the years and my arms ached. I tried to stop the children running all over the place. At the same time I tried to stop the disappointment in me plummeting my hopes like a stone. 'It is small – but cosy. And we're on a bus route. There is a sink and a tap, and there's an electric light,' I said as much to myself as anyone else. 'And Grace will visit once a fortnight. And Baxter too.' Looking around the dingy two rooms I knew how much work it would take to make the dreary sparsely furnished place cosy. I looked around for Willie and inwardly groaned. He'd already gone in next door to introduce himself to the two men. The landlady was telling Donald not to get grubby fingerprints on the walls. Jane was wondering where we were all going to sleep. Mina was saying she was cold. 'And, it's got a good fireplace,' I added, my practised eye flashing over the grate and the brass tile surround. 'And the five children will just have to sleep in one bed.'

'So you're to work in Brooks?' the landlady asked Willie, obviously impressed. He'd come back into the room, a swagger on him and the whiff of beer. I had a nose like a starving animal. I glowered at him but he ignored me. He was standing in the middle of the small room, staring at the cheap furniture as though he too had hoped for something more.

'Oh, aye,' he said, like someone snapping out of a dream, 'aye, that's the place – Brooks of George Street. Fine place. I'm a watchmaker.' He stood as tall as a small man can stand, thrusting out his chest and squaring his shoulders. The woman looked at him in admiration, or so it seemed. Willie had that about him. With his bowler hat and his pocket watch and the way he pronounced certain words. Watchmaker being one. You'd think he was watchmaker to the King himself the way he said it.

'Well, the bairns will have to keep quiet and I'll be wanting the rent every Friday – and if you get into arrears I'll have to chuck ye oot!' She scowled at the children, nodded curtly to faither as she handed him the front door key, then marched out.

'A cup o' tea mother,' Willie said, pocketing the key then placing both hands on the kitchen table. He lowered himself down into a rickety seat. I waited for it to break. So did he the way he sat straight as a poker. When it didn't I took off my coat, put it over the back of another rickety seat, and brought out my pinny. Last thing in the kist, first thing out. I was grateful to bustle. I turned the trickle of water on and was glad for a tap but it was with a heavy heart I filled the kettle.

'Welcome tae Auld Reekie,' Willie said, lifting his tea cup as though it was a dram. The bairns all clapped and ran about the cramped room, bumping into each other and shouting – 'Auld Reekie, Auld Reekie, ye'll have hud yer tea in Auld Reekie.'

'Shhh,' I said harshly, nervous the landlady would throw us out. She lived in the house below and doubtless would hear every word.

'Och, let the bairns hae a wee song,' said faither, placing his black bowler hat on the table. 'It's no everyday you move tae Edinburgh.'

'Aye,' I said, trying to smile and join in the celebration. 'So, here's tae our luck in Edinburgh then.'

'Ach, but the water's no the same as in Haddington,' he said, screwing up his face.

'Oh, well, nothing a wee bit sugar won't sweeten,' I said, frantically. I felt like a sailor bailing water out a sinking ship. Please just stay in and drink tea. Please!

But Willie Lockhart hadn't been over fond of the water all the years in Haddington. It was unlikely to change now we'd reached the great town of Edinburgh.

Mr Walls and Mr Pearson, I found out soon enough, weren't over fond of the water either. Nor did they wear smart brown suits, read books and keep civil tongues in their heads.

It didn't take long for the wee house in Haddington to feel like a mansion in comparison.

13

'If yer old enough tae be running aboot the street,' says mother, 'yer old enough to be giving me a hand.'

Mother was aye working.

'Just coz you're the youngest,' mother says, 'doesnae mean you dinnae get yer wee fingers dirty wi' a bit o' honest work.' She rips an old bed sheet into dusters and hands me one. Jemima's already the wee worker with a scowled face, down on her knees, scrubbing away at the skirting.

I think it will never come to me. I think I'll be running down these scooped stone steps to hold my thumb up in the circle and shout *Eetle ottle black bottle, eetle ottle out* for ever and ever.

I hate work at first, sitting on the floor and rubbing on the big old spoons till I see my face in them when down on the street I hear the bairns turning the long rope and chanting;

House to let
Apply within
A woman put out
For drinking gin!

Then I can't see my face in the spoon because my eyes have filled with tears because skipping is my best thing in the world and I'm not allowed to go down to it.

'Aye, I ken you're just a wee bit thing Johann,' mother says, not moved by my crying, 'but it wisna that long since lassies your age went doon the mines at Newcraighall. And what about these wee boot-blacks on the street, no much bigger than you? So weesht wi the greetin' and think yoursel lucky.'

I don't think mother thinks herself lucky. She's always sighing and when she's at the washing she narrows her eyes so a lump stands out between her eyebrows and her mouth curves down. She's forever wearing a scowl. 'Aye, work Johann – it'll be the death o' me.'

All these women that huddle round the big brown tea-pot in the kitchen say the same thing. They're always moaning about work. Their hands never just sit quiet on their laps. I fall into it, until I'm scrubbing, polishing and dusting with the rest of them.

I'm a worker. That's what mother tells me. 'A rare wee worker,' mother says, seeing me carry the chamber pot downstairs. She hates that job. She takes me up on her knee and says how she cannae abide that filthy stinking job. Then she kisses me on the cheek. I can skip down the stone steps no bother – and if I hold the chamber pot at arm's length the reek doesn't come to me. I'm a grand wee worker.

In the summer the windows are open and people shout from one tenement to another. Chopping neeps for the stew mother carries on a conversation with Mrs Stark across the street. Lungs, even tarred with soot, can fairly bellow.

'Aye, there's a right stushie wi that Pankehurst wifie. But we'll get it.'

'Oh aye Mrs Blackie,' shouts the neighbour, chopping neeps because it's Thursday meaning stew day and everyone gets stew on a Thursday.

'Then tell me this Mrs Stark, wit are we gonna dae wi it?'

'Send yer wee Johanna tae the university – tae be a doctor, ha-ha! – mair like she'd walk on the moon!'

'Aye, and wha's gonna make the denner if it's no us?' Chop, chop, chop. Shout, shout, shout.

'Wha's gonna rub his filthy clothes over the washboard till his hands are red raw?' Chop, chop. 'Wha's gonna ring that mangle till yer hands are red raw and wha's gonna ruin yer eyes wi darning his socks?' Chop, chop, chop.

'Can I get a farthing fir a sweetie?' says I, tugging at mother's skirts and wanting to be out and away from all this shouting and chopping.

'Oot from under my feet bairn,' she says, not lifting her eyes or her knife, 'I'll farthing ye.'

'Can I, please?'

She lays down her knife then scrunches a sheet of faither's newspaper into a ball.

'Now – away an play wi' the ball.' More chopping and sighing.

'An did ye see that bitch Senga's no done the cludgy? Damn disgrace!'

Down the stairs I tear, never giving a thought to the Pankhurst wifie, the university or that bitch Senga. I've no farthing, but I've a ball to toss into the sky.

***

Wee Jane was bright at the school. I knew she would be. They recommended she go to a good school and I tried to get the assistance to pay her way. But no, they said. Your husband works at Brooks in George Street, they said. He earns too much for us to be handing out the assistance to you. 'So where is all this money they tell me you're earning Willie?' I shout, because I'd taken to shouting.

'Don't shriek woman. Who's the one brings in the money? Back to your kitchen and leave off prying into a man's work.'

'But that's just it. You don't bring in the money. Now wee Jane can't go to the good school because – evidently – you earn too much! So where is it?'

'Will ye wheesht? All a man wants is to come home to a quiet house and get a meal in his stomach.'

'Aye, well give me the money to make that meal for your stomach then! Shame on ye, Willie Lockhart! I have to send Jane out with a pillow case. And what does she fill it up wi? Stale bread, that's what. Poor lassie is humiliated, but what can I do? Tell me?'

Willie's wheezing now and strutting about the room. 'It's they toffs in Brooks that dinnae ken a man's worth. I work like a dog and it's they that line their pockets. Aye – go and ask them for the money, why don't you? Go tae their big fancy hooses in Morningside and ask them. Say, what happened tae a' the money Mr Lockhart the watchmaker makes for ye?'

'Hardly,' I said, but I almost felt sorry for him, almost believing he worked like a dog and these fat men in waistcoats and good woollen suits did nothing but drink porter and read papers.

I turned to comfort Jane who was pulling at my skirt, asking about the school. 'No,' I snapped, startling her so much she burst into tears, 'no you can't go to the fancy school. We're workers – and we're poor!'

'Aye, well now,' said Willie, stroking his pocket watch and coughing, 'I wouldn't go as far as to say that. Not poor. No, no, not poor! The Lockharts are not poor.'

Then it was time for Mr Lockhart to perform his one and only domestic duty, the one he performed at five o'clock every day. He carried the soup through from the range and lifted it onto the trivet.

'For what we are about to receive…

War puts an end to working in the big house in the countryside.

But I've a good reference. I find another position. Father wears his look of sore disappointment but I'm nineteen years old, as tall as he –and my mind's set. What can he say?

'Cheerio.' That's all he says, again. 'Cheerio.'

No train for me this time. I take a horse drawn carriage the four miles from Leith to Trinity. Clutching my kist and gazing out to the grimy streets of Leith I try to wipe away that look. I try to harden my heart against him – thinking, God help the British army with a drunkard like Tam Blackie in charge of a bayonet. But it keeps coming back, that look of defeat, his dark eyes like broken glass, a man beaten. I want to cry for him and thousands like him. And I want to hate him for his weakness, for his loud singing, his coarse speech, for slapping mother, for swearing and laughing and drinking in the pub when we sit at home with nothing more than bread and dripping for dinner.

I gaze out at the queues of folk outside shops. Now there's something I haven't seen much of before this war – queues! These days it seems if you want something you have to stand in a line for a good hour at least before you get it. I also notice many of the men on the street are in uniform. I imagine James Melville and how strong and proud he will look in his khaki. And my eyes flit, searching for him, even though I know he has already gone.

I am clutching my fine reference from Grange House. The grand house will be full of officers now and I can hardly bear thinking the state it will be in. I walk up the garden path of this stone house in Edinburgh where I am to be assistant to the cook, and I've to take on the duties of the laundry maid as well. I have the title of general domestic servant. There's a war on, they said in the agency. Count yourself fortunate to find any position. I cast my eye over the outside of the house. It's sandstone and pretty enough, though nothing like as grand as Grange House in Perthshire. Grange House had fiteen bedrooms. This house looks like it has four if it's lucky. I ring the bell and as it clangs through the house I feel my own young heart clanging away with a vengeance. It feels an age I stand there, tugging down my skirt, swallowing hard, looking at the unwashed door-step.

Eventually the door opens and a stout small woman, wearing a stiff hairstyle that I guess is a wig, and a long black dress, stands in the hallway. 'Blackie? Are you Johanna Blackie?' she asks, peering out at me. I nod, and curtsy, all in a fluster, not knowing if this woman who is now staring me up and down is the housekeeper or the lady of the house. In Perthshire it was unheard of for the Balfours to ever answer the door. 'Come away in with you then,' she says, pulling the door back to let me in, 'and be welcome.'

I lift my kist and follow her along the hallway. There's that something in her bearing and dress that tells me this is indeed the lady of the house. She reads my thoughts and turns round at the foot of the stairway. 'Aye then Miss Blackie – you see for yourself. This war's changed the way things were. I lost my servants to the war and hope to goodness you won't be scooting off to wear trousers and join the lassies working in the factories.'

'No ma'am,' I reply, thinking how I worked in Grange House for five years and never once stood face to face talking with Mrs Balfour. Now here I am, in Trinity with Mrs Wakeford not two minutes and you'd think we were the best of chums. Equals even.

'Well, I hope not Johanna, I hope not. You see, I trust my servants, and feed them well, and give them every second Sunday off, after the breakfast things are cleared, that is. And I let them have the pick of our cast offs. Mr Wakeford and I have some bonny clothes I can tell you.' I try not to show the difficulty I have imagining her clothes fitting me. Mrs Wakeford is hardly an inch over five feet and as plump as a pudding. Whereas Grace is forever saying how she can almost fit her hands around my waist.

'Your friend Miss Grace Calder arrives tomorrow. You'll share a room upstairs in the attic and keep it clean. Baxter, the cook, will keep you right. She'll show you the laundry and tell you everything you need to know. And you'll assist her when you've time. It's not like what you've been used to Blackie. There's a war on.' And with that Mrs Wakeford waddles off and leaves me standing in the parlour, wondering what to do next. She must have rung a bell to summon cook because next moment I am face to face with Baxter, red faced and harassed looking like all cooks seem to be. But she smiles and shakes my hand heartily.

'Am I ever pleased to clap eyes on you,' she says, taking my coat off my back then linking her arm in mine and chummily escorting me downstairs. 'A wee cup o' tea Blackie?' she says with a chuckle, as though she's planning on lacing it with brandy.

'Miss Calder will deal wi' the personal care of *them upstairs*,' Baxter tells me when we are both seated at the small servants' table with our hands wrapped around cups of hot tea. She lifts her eyebrows when she mentions 'them upstairs' and I put my hand over my mouth and giggle.

Baxter winks at me then blows over her tea till the brown steaming liquid ripples. 'And you're to do the laundry but wi' this war on you are going to have to turn yer hand to a bit o' this and a bit o' that in addition. I'll need a hand too, of course.' She smiles at me. 'Ye're to be the Jenny a' things.'

I sip my tea, smile at the round faced woman, and nod. She leans towards me and blows over her tea then whispers, 'this war will make spinsters of us all. Mark my words, Blackie. We'll be old maids.'

17 Dovecot Brae
Trinity
Edinburgh
18th October 1915

To Mr James Melville
I have lit the candle and sit here in the night to write to you. There is a nightjar trilling and I swear I heard an owl. I have come to take up a position in a small house in Trinity. It is a pretty place and I will put a little aside each week to have a photograph taken. When we meet the photograph will be for you. There is only me plus cook here, but Grace will come, so three in all and the two old ones upstairs. Grace is to be more a nurse than a lady's maid. Not a day passes I don't think on you, James. I pray wherever you are God protects you. I pray you are alive and is it too presumptious of a servant girl to hope it is to you I may soon give my hand. I am hardly a girl. Almost twenty, heavens. James, I am a good woman and you, I know, are a good man.

Your loving faithful friend
Johanna

Ps – I will send this to the address I have for you in Comrie, in the hope it may find you.

14

Days then weeks pass and though my heart leaps whenever the postman comes to the door there is never a letter for me.

Grace tells me to forget him and to pour my heart and soul into my work. But I can't forget him, and I won't. As the war drags on the kitchen comes to smell more of cabbage and neeps than game and fish. Food is in short supply after the Germans sink the Lusitania. 'Wheat is no getting through Blackie,' Baxter wails. 'We're all going to starve tae death.' She pulls one of her daft faces, supposed to look like a corpse, then she grins. 'Only a wee bit humour will pull us through,' she says, then laughs. I laugh, even though I don't find it funny, and meanwhile think about how I can thin the soup and eek the stores out. For I've grown up with food in short supply. Without knowing it I watched mother make soup from leftovers, peelings and never waste a scrap. So I help Baxter make an ounce of mince go a long way and I can do twenty different things with potatoes, even without the war office giving us 'Potato Pete's' advice.

'Knock-knock?' Baxter says.

I don't know what she's on about. 'Excuse me?' I say.

Baxter laughs that loud laugh of hers. 'It's a joke, silly. I say, knock-knock and now you've to say, who's there then when I answer you put who on the end.' So she starts over and this time I say, who's there.

'Boo,' she says.

'Boo who,' I say, and that starts her chuckling.

'Don't cry, Johanna,' she says, holding her sides with laughter.

It feels good to laugh, even if there is a war on. And even if I don't understand all cook's jokes. 'Now, Blackie,' she says, 'with your handsome man off fighting the Huns you need cheering up.' It is the onions I am chopping making me cry, but still I nod through my tears. And so she says how there was this young tramp went knocking on the back door of a big house asking for food and the cook answered and said – you should go to the Front and the tramp said, I did but nobody heard me so I came round here. 'Get it, Blackie?' she says, waiting for me to roar with laughter. I bite my lip, trying to see what's funny. 'The Front,' she says, beaming a wide smile, 'that's where the soldiers go. The war.'

'Oh,' I say then I put down my sharp knife and laugh, mainly because Baxter is laughing and it feels good once I start.

'You have to laugh,' Baxter says, 'else we'd be down on our knees weeping.'

In addition to helping Baxter in the kitchen I wash the pots and the plates. I stew the prunes and run the messages. I help Grace lay the fires because as housekeeper-cum-ladies-maid-cum-nurse she has more than enough to do, and besides, after Grange House I am something of a fire making expert and can have them cleared, black- leaded, polished with a cloth dipped in paraffin then set for lighting in next to no time.

And despite the fact Baxter sighs and says, 'there's a war on Blackie,' at least ten times a day it's all fairly quiet on the home front in leafy Trinity on the gentle north slopes of Edinburgh. No letter comes from James. He is in France, doing his duty. Not a night goes by I don't put up a prayer for him.

***

'...may the Lord make us truly thankful.'

Being head of the household it was for Willie to speak the prayer. Then we ate, me feeding two or three bairns. He noisily drinking back his bowlful. Then he'd retire to the seat over at the coal fire and smoke his pipe. If a good mood was on him the bairns would get a ghost story, or a tune on the fiddle, or a few words read out from the book he called his other bible – The Ragged Trousered Philanthropists. Then out he'd go, or, if he had no coin in his pocket, he'd visit the lodgers in the room next door.

I didn't like to go to sleep before Willie was in at night. I'd get the children settled around eight o'clock then nod off in the chair, but with half an eye open for Willie on the stair. This night I was ready for bed but had nodded off in the chair in front of the fire. Next thing I heard loud singing in the stairwell. *'I didnae go to nae sic school!'* I sat up, bewildered, wondering where I was. The next moment the door swung open and Willie made his entrance, just as the clock struck midnight. '*Tae play the fool.*' He saluted the clock then lurched across the room, humming tunelessly and swinging his arms back and forth as though conducting an orchestra of ghosts. I jolted to my feet and set about guiding him through to the bed. I'd had plenty practice, arm under his elbow, my shoulder bearing the weight of him. With all my strength I could usually manage to steer him to safety, but he pitched away from me. He fell on the bairns and woke wee Donald. 'Let the laddie sleep for heaven's sake faither,' I wailed, trying to prize his fingers off the wee laddie. But Willie held fast. 'For the love o' God,' I hissed, 'leave the laddie.'

'Wheesht, jist a wee song. A man's got tae hae some comfort. If his ain prudish wife won't gie it.' He flung me a cold haggard look. 'Sing 'Ca' The yowes' for your faither son,' he slurred, stroking the boy's face.

So Donald got out of bed and sung at midnight with a sputtering candle for light and by his side his drunken father, weeping.

Ca' the yowes, tae the knowes
Ca' them whaur the heather grows
Ca' them whaur the burnie rowes,
My bonnie dearie.

The song done, Donald stole back into bed. 'The song's finished faither, come now,' I said, using the soothing voice that sometimes worked. I slipped his coat off him then bent down to unlace his boots and lower him onto the bed.

'Wheesht, you auld cow,' he snapped, as though he was suddenly aware of me loosening his boot laces. 'A man's got tae have his song. And a wife's tae dae her duty. Fine paps mother.' He tugged at my nightgown.

'Did I ever tell ye, how ye've got a fine pair o paps.' I pulled away but Willie, for all his drunkenness, was strong. I heard my old nightgown rip. I felt his clammy hands grasp at my breasts. 'Oh, aye,' he was panting hard now, 'fine paps.'

There's not as much as a sliver of moon.

I can't sleep. I'm turning on my side, then onto my back. Lizzie's puttering snores are like wind in the barley, bending the sheaves back and forth. I can't see a thing. She might be James Melville. It might be his breath rising and falling. It's a warm night. I push the rough blanket aside. The heavy cotton of my nightgown rides up. It has twisted round me. I tug at it. I would like a new soft nightgown. I've seen the mistress in her fine nightgown. She glides about on the landing, her flaxen hair unpinned and flowing all the way down her back and her not caring a fig who sees. My hair is black. My gown is cambric. Hers is silk. I imagine he is here with me, James Melville, in this attic room. He strokes my cheek. I gaze into his gentle eyes. They are like skies with endless hope. He strokes my neck, James Melville does. With the soft tip of his middle finger he traces the first letter of my name on the front of my neck. He writes on my throat. J. We have that in common. J, for Jesus, for Johanna, for James – and joy. His finger travels round to my collar bone, my shoulder, and back to my neck. I gasp. Lizzie grunts and moves. 'Lizzie?' I whisper. She doesn't answer. Then his finger strokes down and down. He brushes my breasts.

I whimper in the night.

15

'Now that's what I call a Sunday white.' That was Mrs Greig, holding up one of the shirts she took in for washing. She was right. She brought it up like snow.

'But would ye tak a look at this blood. Damn fool nicked himself shaving. I've tried salt, soda. I've tried scrubbing with borax till my arm ached. But will the damned spot shift? Will it hell!' That was Mrs Hannay. She was very particular. Och, you're seeing things, we always told her, but she was having none of it. 'Blood is blood, once spilt there's no getting rid of it.'

'Ach that's nothing, see that brown sauce stuff? He dribbles it down his shirt doesn't he? I says to him, I says Stewie, it's a bib you're needing so you are. He thought I was joking. Laughed like a bairn. Oh but no Stewie, says I, I am being serious. He's worse than a bairn. I tell you that man'll sit there wi' a bib on if it's the last thing he does.' That was Mrs Mason. Behind her back the women in the steamie said Mr Mason's hen-pecked and the way they said it you knew there was no worse thing for a man to be.

I was coming back from the steamie in South Gray's Close, pushing a pram full of clean laundry piled high. It was already beginning to get dark. There was a spring to my step after a whole day's company. Heating panfuls of water in the kitchen took forever and lugging buckets all over the place was back breaking work. The new wash houses were a God send. They had as much hot water as you needed and all the best wringers and mangles a woman could wish for. And there was always a good blether to be had. We didn't only talk about cleaning. We'd get on to the bairns and the old days, and the new films, not that I'd seen any but the way the other women retold the films, with all the arm movements and expressions on their faces, and the way they changed their voices, I felt as if I had. Just listening to the women in the steamie I swear I had died and kissed a prince and ridden bare-back on a horse, danced at fine balls and sailed on tall ships. It was Ben Hur this and Charlie Chaplin that.

The street lights were coming on. I had Jane walking beside me and wee Gordon bundled up in all the clean laundry. I was hurrying through Newington back towards Montague Street when a cold shiver ran over my skin. I looked up. I saw a drunk man staggering down the lane towards me. I steered the pram to the other side of the lane. 'Who's that mammy?' Jane said, running to keep up with me.

'Nobody we ken,' I told her, pulling her right close to me, 'come on.'

'But mammy, the man's falling down. It's…'

I pulled her away. 'Dinnae stare. It's rude. It's nobody we know. It'll be right dark soon and look at us – the tea not even done.'

'But mammy,' she cried, 'it's grand-dad.'

I stared at the man. He was on the ground by this time, lit in a sickly pool of lamp-light, one arm reaching out towards me. His face was all puffed up and threaded with purple and red broken veins. His eyes blood-shot. His voice a slur, lifting off the cobbles. 'It's me!' he called out, 'Tam. Yer ain faither.' I was shaking and trying to steer the pram around him. He tried to grab at my ankle. 'Yer ain blood.' He hit out at the wheel of the pram. The bairn was wailing now. 'Aye, yer ain kin, him that walked a' they miles sho you'd get shomething to eat. Yer ain faither!' He was lying on the street, staring up at me.

I staggered backwards, lifted Jane up into the pram and hurried past, the washing almost toppling off. I fumbled into my pocket. All I had was a threepenny bit and I needed that to buy bread and milk. I stopped then ran the few steps back to where my own father lay sprawled on the ground. I was scared he would lash out. Quickly I bent down and set the coin in front of him. 'That's all I've got,' I muttered then turned and hurried away.

Jane kept on at me – 'what's the matter with grandpa? It was grandpa, wasn't it?' Don't ask questions, that's what I told her. Ask no questions, get no lies. It was easier that way.

After that she stopped asking – why she can't go to the good school? Why her father falls onto the floor? Why her mammy has holes in her shoes? Why she eats stale bread soaked in water?

She didn't ask but she knew. I watched her lift her head night after night when the knock came to the door. The – Mrs Lockhart your husband's drunk on the street, would you come and get him – knock. My ten year old daughter watched as I put on my old coat, my brow knitting. 'You should be asleep,' I said. And shouldn't have to watch your own father lifted in to bed, I didn't say.

How many times I put on my coat to go out into the night and pick my husband off the street? I wasn't the only one. It would have been considered heartless to leave him to freeze to death. Well, heartless I had grown. For one night I left him there and hoped he would die in the cold and he might well have if somebody on the street didn't take pity on him and help him up the stairs.

'Somebudy cares,' he said as the man helped him in. Willie staggered through to the bed and fell on it. I didn't look up from my sewing. I waited a few minutes then went through and pulled off his boots, the reek of damp sour feet hitting me.

Sometimes, when he had fallen asleep after I had talked him out of getting the knife, I'd lie sobbing, the pillow dampening under my face. Often then I heard one of the children, Jane or Donald, whisper in the darkness – 'it's alright mammy, we're here, it's alright!'

And there were nights when the only solace was to write.

13/5 Montague Street
Edinburgh
24th May 1931

My dear James

It is pigeons we have here and starlings. What a din they make in the day, though now it is dead of night. Someone is shouting out on the street. Not my father, I pray. Oh, James, sometimes I think fate has written that a poor girl such as I cannot expect a good and proper love. My father was drunk in the street. My husband is too often drunk in the street. Perhaps my grandfather and grandfather before him were drunk in the street. Is that my fate? Will it go on this way, for ever and ever? Or can I hope for something better? I swear as God is my witness, my own bairns will not fall drunk in the street. These letters I write to you hope for more, but I know you don't receive the letters. And perhaps you are cold in the grave. But I can hope. And pray. And continue to tell you of my heart, and sometimes simply prattle.

The air here is thick with smoke from a thousand coal fires and that's why they call this town Auld Reekie. For you see, we have flitted. I am not sorry to put Haddington behind me though the pity is it's a cramped wee place we've come to.

But let me not dwell on that.

It is again Victoria Day, or it was for midnight has come and gone. I was just fifteen that sun filled blessed day I met you and so very shy. You took my hand and steadied the boat and some magic I now know to be love came into me then, and though the road for me since has not been an easy one, there is still a light strong in me. That light is largely due to you, James. And the bairns too.

I walk for you. I walk towards you, not away. No, I walk with you. It is as if you are in me wherever I go. I am not the gay girl I was. There are threads of silver in my hair and an expression that eats into my face. Like a portrait painter had etched lines to alter my youth, and like he is trying with his art to hide my disappointment, but he does not succeed.

There was no holiday for me this Victoria Day. I have five children and when I said to my husband maybe we could have an outing he scowled and reminded me old Victoria is dead and the toffs might take holidays but not the working man.

There was so much cherry blossom that day. Some fell in my hair and I remember feeling like a bride and you were the groom. I blush to say these words but does it matter now? It is too late.

My heart aches
Johanna xxx

16

It's 1900 and I'm to start at the school.

I get a grey cotton smock made by my mother, and black lace-up boots. That Sunday night I sit in heated water in the tin bath in front of the fire and get the comb tugged through my hair till all the beasties are gone. I get my nails pared with a pen knife. 'Ye're a bonnie wee thing right enough,' mother says, slapping my bottom for being a bonnie wee thing. 'Don't go making eyes at the boys.' Father laughs and winks at me while mother goes on fussing, 'we're respectable mind,' and I think we are.

I don't know that my lovely new smock has been a bed sheet, or that our furniture's held together by rags. I don't know it isn't respectable for your father to sing out loud at midnight and fall with a crash to the ground while your own mother cries into a glass of beer. I don't know other folk have blankets on the bed instead of clothes. All I know is I'm off to the school and my long black hair is in pigtails and upon my head is a lovely ivory-white bonnet.

I love walking up the road and hearing my boots go smack-smack on the pavement. The boots have a tongue that rubs up against my ankle. The boots were Jemima's and they're too big for me. They make me walk funny but still I feel like a toff. Half the bairns in the school don't have any shoes or boots but I do, even though mostly, at first, I take them off – to skip and jump peevers and play 'I sent a letter to my love' when we go into the playground.

I want to send a letter. I don't know what a letter is. A, B and C says Miss Macdonald. The girls sit on the left side of the classroom and the boys on the right. For playtime we go to different playgrounds – so I don't make eyes at any boys. We sit on long hard wooden benches and even though your bum hurts you're not allowed to squirm about. Sitting up straight is the first thing we're taught and I think Miss Macdonald says it twenty times a day. Not to me though. I sit up ram rod straight.

We have to keep our eyes on the teacher's pointer. The windows in the classroom are high up so you can't look outside except to a square patch of sky. But I don't mind about that. I love looking at the teacher. She always wears a long dark grey dress all the way to the floor and over it a starched white apron. I thought all women work in houses and sit round big brown teapots and chop neeps for soup and hang out the washing. Miss Macdonald is a wonder to me – she works in a school and speaks nice and smiles and her voice has a soft ring in it.

'Very good Blackie,' she is always saying and sometimes the other children snigger. They say Blackie means clarty and I must come from a right dirty family. I wish I was called Macdonald. I've got jet black hair. I am the seventh child. And my name is Blackie. I am feared I am a witch. Jemima says if I sing hymns and hold the bible I'll be protected from all evil. There's a lot of hymn singing in the school, and a lot of prayers. I sing All things Bright and Beautiful louder than anyone.

Miss Macdonald's long dress trails to the ground so with every step she takes, past the long rows of us bairns, her dress makes a swishing sound, like wind through the long grass. Swish-swish. Swish-swish.

The teacher wears her long hair pinned up in a soft bun at the nape of her neck. I think she looks like the queen. Q for queen. M for Miss Macdonald. From the day I start at the school I love her. I want to do everything right for her. She's very particular about handwriting. 'Forming your letter beautifully, girls and boys will get you on in life,' she says. Then she looks at my slate. 'Take that B for Blackie,' she says, bending her face so close to mine I can smell the soap on her skin, 'and give it a straight spine. That will make you really look like somebody fine. Somebody proper.'

I practise my letters over and over again. We are all to write a letter to Miss Macdonald and give it to her. She gets forty black slates piled up on her desk. It's the first letter I have ever written.

Dear Miss Macdonald
I love you
From Johanna

'Who is Johanna?' she says, smiling. I put my hand up. I am somebody fine and proper. 'Ah! Blackie!' she says, 'thank-you.'

***

The clipped English voice crackled into the small room in Montague Street. 'A quarter of the British work force unemployed,' the voice said. 'Hardest hit are the heavy industries; coal, mining, steel and ship-building.'

'Guid thing I'm a watch-maker,' Willie said. We were all listening to the newscast on a wireless that Willie had brought home, in exchange for a bit o' watch-mending. 'Oh aye,' he went on, 'a fine trade for a man, but wi a' they lines o' gaunt faced jobless men lookin for a handout, they're no wanting watches mended.'

'Pity these poor folks,' I said.

'Pity?' said Willie, getting up and spreading his arms wide, 'pity? It's a revolution that's needed. A bloody rising. Not pity!'

Willie had been with his two cronies, the bachelors. They drank, smoked and talked Bolshevik rebellions. 'Aye, vive la revolution,' he said, punching the air then he burst into a verse of *Red Wave the banners-O.*

Young Jamesy was up at the table trying to get a tune out of a piece of paper and a comb. Jane, the oldest, was knitting herself a red scarf with wool I'd unravelled from an old cardigan. Donald was sketching a picture of the clock and Mina was fiddling with the knob on the wireless, now that the newscast was over, and trying to find the new dance music. Then Willie lurched next door again – for some proper communist talk, he said, slamming the door behind him. It wasn't long before the three of them sailed back through the room, crooning all, *Ten for the works o' Lenin O,* and out, into the night.

Wee Gordon sat on my knee and I sang '*Wee willie winkie*' over and over. When that song was done he cried for another one. *Ally Bally*, I suddenly sang. He gurgled and looked like the happiest wee boy in the world. *A peen to see the puppet show*, and as I sang that small dingy room became the room in Gordon Street. And there were not 70,000 Scottish soldiers dead and buried in the fields of France and Flanders. I felt myself slip into memories. All I had to do was bat an eyelid, hear the strain of an old tune, see the light hit the window in a certain long-gone shimmering fashion and I was back. But what good would memories do me? Just gives the lassie that bit further tae fall! I stopped singing. What was the use in dreaming? James Melville was in a boat and rowing away. I could only see his back. He was getting smaller and smaller. I snapped out of it. Gordon was pulling at my sleeve and begging for another song. *I loved a soldier, a Scottish soldier…* I sang, but Gordon didn't like that song. He wanted another one. Maybe because my voice was breaking.

I told myself no woman could be luckier. I looked over to young Jamesy, up at the table with his home-made mouth-organ. He lifted his head and grinned at me, his blonde hair flopping into his eyes.

There was nothing like the bairns for blowing away the cold wind. Jane, at her knitting, laughed too and Donald, at his sketching, laughed, and Mina, her ear pressed up against the wireless said, 'will you lot belt up. I can't hear my song!'

For maybe two hours we sat like that, warm in the company of each other. Though there was an edge to that warmth. I could see it in the bairn's faces. I could hear it in the rise to my voice.

> '*Burke is the butcher and Hare's the thief*
> *Knox is the man who eyes the beef!*'

I ran to the door, peering down in the darkness to the rabble on the stairs. 'What a hulla-balloo! Keep the noise down for the love o' goodness,' my own voice an urgent muffled cry. Three or four men, having conquered the three flights of stone steps, lurched forward and fell into the kitchen. The bachelors made a futile attempt to sober up in my company and the other man whom I'd never seen before grasped his cap and bowed, so low I thought he had keeled over. 'This, mister Mahoney, is ma mansion hoose,' said Willie, hoisting the man up by his jacket and now the two of them were swaying from side to side. I felt sea-sick just looking at them, all pitching and tipping. By this time the red faced Mahoney was surveying the pokey room with admiration, his eyes wide as saucers. 'Tea mither,' commanded Willie, lowering himself into a seat at the table and taking out his pipe which promptly fell on the floor. For want of another chair Mahoney squatted down on the floor next to Willie. 'This fine working man here, comrade Mahoney by name – would ye credit it – lives in a one-roomed hoose wi' nae window,' Willie slurred, leaning over and patting the fine working man on the back. 'Not a sun beam, not a lamp post, not a passing cloud, och no, no even a smattering of rain for a view. Nae windae for comrade Mahoney.'

Mr Mahoney was weeping with the concern. 'And these – are my bairns,' said Willie, flinging his arm out in the direction of the wireless. His bairns all turned to glower at the spectacle and I saw how their faces darkened, their eyes narrowed. Only Mina looked at her father with pity. She kept her ear pressed up against the wireless and turned the volume up. My heart lurched seeing her trying to put up this wall to make everything all right. A crackling rendition of 'Blue Moon' spat into the room. I glared at the bachelors and made no move to put the kettle on. The bachelors, looking uncomfortable, muttered something about retiring to their room next door but Willie was having none of it. Instead he turned and beckoned to Jamesy.

'Ma son,' he shouted, with a punch to the air as though he was fighting a ghost. 'Ma ain laddie Wullie. Ma namesake.' His namesake was twisting his hands together. My heart went out to the poor laddie and his confusion.

'Leave him be,' I cried. But Willie, with a great flourish, pulled a ten shilling note from his pocket.

'See if I die Wullie son,' said father, grabbing wee Jamesy by the wrist and pulling him towards him. I knew what that reeking breath would smell like on the poor boy's face. I knew what that hot grasping hand round his small wrist felt like. I ran to pull him away and Willie, more on the ball than I thought, kicked out his foot. I tripped over it and fell headlong onto the floor. 'Wheesht mither. This is men's business.'

From where I lay, my face level with Mr Mahoney's tackety boot I heard Mina's wireless – *you heard me saying a prayer for.* I got up quick. Now wee Gordon was crying. I saw his face redden and hands harden into fists, ready to box with his own father. Donald was at my side but Willie heeded none of this. 'If I'm taken frae this world and wha kens but it could be any day, 'he sniffed, 'tak this money, son, and look after mother. Ye're the man o' the hoose son.' Stuffing the crumpled ten shilling note in the boy's hand Willie staggered up. Linking his arm under Mr Mahoney's the drunken party sailed over choppy seas to the bachelor's room, Mahoney sobbing at Willie's impending death. 'Let us partake o a little something gentlemen,' said Willie, 'tae sweeten the dreams and soften the end.' And off they went, *without a dream in my heart, without a love of my own.*

I watched Jamesy reach up to the tin I kept at the back of the sugar jar.

'Bed now,' I said, thinking how we'd have meat pies with gravy the next day, and how I would bake a cake, and buy oranges and nuts and eggs, and fresh bread.

17

I can hear the postman's whistle on the stairs.

By the time I hear his knock at the door my heart is fit to burst. I run to answer the door. Mother is down at the cludgy and father has gone to work. With a good many thank-yous I take the letter with the agency sealing wax stamped on the back. With shaking hands and thumping heart I open it, hiding myself in the shadow behind the door.

I draw out the yellow parchment paper and hold it up close. I bite my lip and hold myself still. I'm to call in at the agency at the very next opportunity, the letter says. The lady at the agency wishes to have a look at me but – judging by my handwriting she is impressed and all being in order I will be just the one to fit the position. Tears sting at my eyes.

I hear the front door creak open. 'Mother!' I step out from the shadow. 'I've got a position. And I'm going away.'

'Aye? Well, good for you Johann. I never fancied being a servant myself but no doubt you're suited to it. Yer faither's no going to think much o' it though.'

I search mother's face for traces of regret. She's lugged up a bucket of water from the stand pipe. She places it on the kitchen floor and sighs. Is she sorry her youngest child is leaving home? 'Dinnae fash yersel – I'll tell him,' she says. 'Aye hen, you'll do them proud, they high falutin folk wi' their fancy ways. You're a good worker.'

I want to hug mother when she says that but I don't know how to. So I just stare at her. She looks old and tired, and if she's sad to be losing me, her wee Princess, she doesn't show it. She dips a rag in the water and wrings it out then sets to wiping her work board. 'We'll appreciate a bit o' yer wages. Send it wi' the post,' she says not stopping her vigorous wiping. 'What wi' faither not keeping so great, it'll help.'

But mother isn't drunk now, just tired. She pauses in her work and looks at me. 'Aye, aye, lassie – wit's in store fir ye, eh? Just mind – work hard – that's how ye get on, and dinnae forget us.' Then, as though she suddenly spots a stain on the workboard she plunges her rag into that bucket of ammonia and water and wrings it out with a vengeance, muttering, 'and ye're as guid as them, remember that. We're a' Jock Tamson's bairns.' But whether mother believes that or not, I can't tell.

***

We'd not been in Montague Street a year and a half when Willie announced, 'I'm no going tae bother wi' that fancy Brooks ony mair.' It was a Friday night and the pay packet was not forthcoming. Willie had just finished his soup. We stopped eating and all held our big round spoons in mid-air so the Scotch Broth dripped back into the bowls.

'What?' I felt the blood drain from my face.

'I says, I'm no going tae work fir ony man and specially no that toff Brook. It's no right for a communist tae kow-tow tae they fat port-drinking toffs. So, I'm ma ain man. I'll go round the hooses and mend their watches, them that have got watches for mending.'

I shook my head. I lost all appetite for finishing that broth even though I was hungry. Destitute; that was the word that threatened me. But Willie was looking fair pleased with himself. 'A man, let me tell you bairns, has got tae be his ain man. Come the Revolution they'll be nae mair toffs getting fat on the labours o' the workin' man.' Willie was even enjoying this. A disaster that he turned to his own hand. 'Mina,' he said, his round face beaming with triumph, 'gie us Burns hen. Up and gie us the guid words.'

So wee Mina stood, knowing the guid words her father meant:

You see yon Birkie ca'd a lord
Wha struts an stares an a' that

Tho' hundreds worship at his word
He's but a coof fir a' that.'

'Guid lassie, guid. Coof! Ha! I like that. And Willie Lockhart is no working for ony mair coofs. I am ma ain man!'

I said nothing. I cleared up the soup bowls and didn't look at him. He moved to his seat by the fire, fair pleased with himself and his revolution. I heard him shake out his 'Daily Worker.' After the clearing up was done I took the folded letter from the box. I was looking for the right time and this was it. I'd wipe that smile off his face.

I went through with the letter in my hand. Something had snapped inside me. As though a barn door had come unhinged and was banging in the wind, all these things I kept held in were pushing out. I hardly trusted my mouth. My lips were trembling.

'Then wit's this?' I said. It was all I could do not to shout. 'This? This?' I repeated, my voice breaking. He looked up. For a second I saw a shadow of fear in his red-rimmed eyes. I said it again. 'Wit's this? Notice tae quit – that's wit it is.' I didn't even keep my voice to a hush for the sake of the bairns. I didn't care anymore. 'Ye've no paid the rent. Brook's no pay ye for the past two months – eh? The coofs go and sack ye did they? Wit now Mr Lockhart? The poorhouse?'

Still pulling on his clay pipe Willie glared down into the Daily Worker. I was shaking, the letter in my hand flapping like a leaf in the wind. Willie drew out a bottle of stout from under his chair. 'Well?' I screamed. 'We can't go back to Gordon Street.' I wanted to knock that bottle of beer from his hand, like I did to my own father, years back. I wanted to drop to my knees and howl. But five children were watching me. I could hear their little gasps. My heart went out to them. I said it again, quieter this time. 'We can't go back to Gordon Street.' And the letter dropped from my hand.

Of course we couldn't go back to Gordon Street. Hadn't I tried that? We couldn't go to Grace, or Baxter, or Jemima. 'So where too, faither?' I said, my voice breaking, 'where in the name o' God are we to go?'

Willie shrugged his shoulders, drained the bottle of stout and stood up. 'I'll go and see somebody. I've got comrades.' And off he went.

'Och no rush, Mrs Lockhart,' said the landlady, her of the broom-handle-banged-on-the-ceiling five nights out of seven. She stood in the kitchen, her kitchen, careful not to step on a child. They were under her skirt playing marbles with pebbles on the floor. 'Och no,' she said, 'I wouldn't see you on the street wi' all these wee ones. Give me the money soon as you get it Mrs Lockhart and meanwhile be looking around. I'm a good Christian and wouldn't have you out on the streets. But all the same, I can't be having arrears. It's no a charity I'm running here.'

It isn't only my father that's drunk.

Half the time mother is too. My own parents! It shames me to see them clinking their jars together, toasting this, that and the next thing – each thing more ridiculous. Here's tae the wee mannie that bakes the breid! Aye, an here's tae that damn creaky bed! Oh aye, an here's tae that lazy bitch Senga wha doesnae dae her bit tae clean the cludgy! Wit are ye toasting her fir? Aye, right enough, here's no tae Senga! Ha-ha! An here's no tae the cludgy! Here's tae bonnie Scotland an a' wha' work in her! Here's tae us, wha's like us, damn few and they're a' deid!

And if it isn't glasses clinking and a wee bit dance round the kitchen it's mother banging her fist on the table and glowering at father. 'Yer nothin' but a damn tattie howker,' she says, then he's banging his fist on the table till the table legs creak and I'm scared the table is going to break and he's slurring, 'Aye well? That's a damn shight better than shovelling horse-shite that's fir shure.'

I look for my chance to tell them I don't like the shoe shop and I want to do something different. I think maybe when they're both in good moods, dancing round the kitchen, will be the best time. There's never a good time.

***

While I was looking for rent money Willie disappeared. He did now and again and though I worried about him the peace in the house and the way the bairns all relaxed meant I didn't worry that much. He took his battered old violin, put on his dusty bowler hat and off he went. 'The Ragged Trousered Philanthropists,' stuffed in his pocket. Sometimes he disappeared for weeks on end.

'Where's faither?'

'Begging in the streets of Paris. Playing his fiddle in Clydeside. Mending watches for the good King Edward. Gone to his beloved Bolsheviks.'

'But where is he really?'

'I don't know!'

'Well good riddance to him,' Donald said, banking up the coal fire.

'Wheesht now. You can't speak like that about yer faither.'

'It's true.'

'Stop that Donald and make yer mother a cup of tea.' I shook my head at the laddie, sat down by the fire and put my feet up.

'Aye mother. I'll treat you. And I'll treat you well.' And the nine year old boy spooned tea leaves into the large brown metal tea-pot.

'Two sugars Donald,' I said, playing along as though we were right proper somebodies in the tea-rooms in Princes Street with not a care in the world.

'Now would madam wish fir a biscuit to go along with her tea?'

'Well now, a biscuit would be a fine thing. Reach up into the tin and you might find a broken biscuit there. And Donald can have one too.'

'Oh no madam, I'm the waiter. You're the lady.'

So Donald brought me a cup of tea. The house was fine and still. I sighed and stretched my legs out. Even though we were to leave this house, even though for all I knew my husband could be lying dead in a ditch somewhere, I felt at peace.

'Lift the plate up nice then use tongs to lift the biscuit off properly,' I said.

'Does madam want two bits o' biscuits?'

'No butler, one will suffice nicely, thank you.'

'You're pretty, mother,' he said, placing the broken biscuit on my plate.

'You know what they say about all work and no play?' Donald shook his head. 'Well,' I went on, 'work steals beauty away. See these hands o' mine son – red raw with work. And there's grey in this black hair. Once, aye, once I looked fine.' I paused then rushed on. 'I had a photograph done once.'

'Did you mother?'

'Aye, when I was young.'

'Where is it now mother?'

I've seen the photographer's studio on Hanover Street up town.

Once a month we are given a Saturday half day holiday so this Saturday I've booked myself a sitting at the studio. I have saved for three months, now here I am, groomed and feeling excited, like a bairn going to Portobello beach. I try to slip out the house without Mrs Wakeford seeing me but no such luck.

'Have a nice afternoon off, Blackie. You are looking very smart. Going somewhere special?'

'Um – no, not really ma'am.'

'Not really but nonetheless a bit special. Is that it Blackie? You can tell your mistress I hope.' Grace is clipping Mrs Wakeford's finger nails and glances briefly up at me. I can tell by the way her eyebrows lift that she's impressed.

'Yes, ma'am,' I say, blushing.

'Well?'

'Well – it's the – um, photographers ma'am. I don't have one. A photograph that is. And –and I thought I could have one. Ma'am.'

'Well, Johanna,' she says, 'you must wear a hat. Not seemly for unmarried girls to show off their heads. And sit demure Blackie – these photographs last for a long time you know.'

'Yes ma'am.'

'I mean Johanna, you could be dead and your children will look at this photograph years from now and how will they feel if their own dead mother is hatless?'

'Yes ma'am. Quite. Probably unhappy, ma'am.'

'Quite. And Blackie – if you could be back by tea time Mr Wakeford would appreciate his Sunday collar starched.'

'But – right. Yes ma'am.'

'A photograph only takes an hour. I know Blackie. I've had several done. Oh! And Blackie.'

'Yes, ma'am?'

'Don't smile. Smiling cheapens the photograph. You don't want to live to regret an awful glaikit smile.'

'I won't, ma'am.'

Then I am off, hair washed, blouse and skirt flat-ironed and wearing the brown felt hat Mrs Wakeford recommended. I have to hurry now, and have to walk the three miles into town. Every farthing is needed for the photograph.

After an age I arrive at the studio. I compose myself, breathe deeply, open the door and step inside.

'Miss Blackie?'

I nod, heart thudding, knees trembling. With my handkerchief I gently dab at the perspiration on my forehead.

'Lovely to see you. Good day to you. A very good-day indeed. Now, come away into the forest,' the man in a black frock coat says, smiling so his heavy handle-bar moustache lifts all the way to his round red cheeks.

I am on a wooden bench in a woodland setting. I hold my face at an angle to the left, my chin slightly pointing down but my eyes toward the box camera. He has the box balanced on a tripod and surrounded by reams of black cloth, like a mourning dress. I have been sitting like this for ages and my shoulders are sore. He has told me three times that if I move even half an inch the photograph will spoil. 'We want you preserved untarnished,' he says. 'A work of beauty is alive for ever.' He speaks like the poets. He has given me a sheet of paper to hold leisurely in my lap.

'Imagine Europe is at peace,' he says, like a minister in the church. Then he winks at me. 'And imagine, Miss Blackie, that you are holding a love letter in your hand,' and the way he speaks and the cloth of painted trees at my back and my hair smelling so fresh, it's easy to imagine a love letter. Mr James Melville rows into my mind, but I have forgotten what he looks like. I see only his back, his strong shoulders and his broad arms, rowing away from me. I hardly dare breathe.

'Watch the birdie,' the man in front of me, now hidden behind black cloth, shouts out, waving a stuffed bird above his head.

Then blinding lightning flashes!

'Och. Shame. I do believe you blinked Miss Blackie. Never mind – we'll try again. Now don't move a muscle. The art of stillness and patience, Miss Blackie, is the greatest of all the arts. If we could all but be still there would be no need to fight. Now then, let me just sort this contraption. Imagine you are dreaming – after reading the love letter.'

I am blushing but it is easier not to move if I let myself dream. So I do – and there I am in my own wee house and there are bairns playing at my feet and there's a good man singing to them and I can smell a rich meat pie cooking and the place is gleaming. Mother, that's what they're calling me. Mother...

'The photograph, mother, where is it?'

I shook my head, and smiled at him, my bonnie wee laddie. 'In the kist.'

'Can I see it?'

'You won't know me.' I put my tea cup down on the floor. 'Well, sit quiet and I'll see if I can find it. We don't want to wake wee Gordon up.'

The house was quiet. The bachelors were out. Jane, Mina and Jamesy were down on the street playing. I could hear their shouts and verses drift up. *Tam, Tam, the gundy man, washed his face in the frying pan…* So I fumbled in the kist, pretending to myself I didn't know exactly where the photograph was. My fingers curled round the hard edge of the frame. I lifted it up through the linen sheets with a tenderness as though it was my own young, dreaming self I was resurrecting.

'Here,' I said, folding back the tissue paper. 'That's me.' I lowered the photograph into Donald's open palms.

For a while he said nothing. I eased myself back into the chair and watched him gaze at that young lass he held in his hands. 'You're beautiful mother,' he said, 'right beautiful.'

'That's enough now,' I said, 'I better put it back.'

'You've got a letter in your hand mother.'

'Not really son.'

'But it looks like one. And you are so pretty. Like a Queen. See your blouse and young face. It looks like a love letter you've got there.'

'Well, it's not.' I got up then and took it from him.

I bent over the kist, tears pricking my eyes. I fumbled through the towels and bed sheets. I wanted to bury it deep. 'It's not,' I murmured, piling sheet after sheet on top of her.

18

Two weeks later, as though he had only popped out for a bottle of milk, Willie came home, bleary eyed, swinging his battered violin case and both he and it looking the worse for wear. A few more words of French spiced up his speech now. 'Liberte! Egalite! Fraternity!' he shouted before looking round the house with the confused expression of someone wondering where he was.

'Where were you faither?' I asked him, looking up from my board where I was busy scrubbing potatoes.

He spun round and stared at me. For a second it was as if he had forgotten who I was.

'Playing the fiddle for the workers of France, that's where.' And he plonked himself into the chair by the fire, 'and damn the exploitative capitalists!'

'And the rent money, Willie? And a place to live? Did you find a place for your family to live with the workers in France?'

'Woman,' he snapped, flashing his rheumy eyes at me. He was angry I could tell. He was tired. He had probably walked for miles. Doubtless he had hardly slept. He was fired up with the revolution and the last thing he wanted was a nagging wife cutting him down to size. But I cared nothing for his revolution. He'd have us sleeping on the street, reciting poetry. He was only back ten minutes and the sight of him deflated me. Suddenly the peace was shattered and the reality of the situation was back. He had found no rent money. He had not bothered himself to find a place for his family to stay.

'Even if we sleep under a whin bush on Arthur's Seat,' he said, 'we'll kow-tow tae nae toffs.'

The drink was well in him. I knew how it went. This could last for weeks. Then every rousing Scots song would get an airing and the fiddle would bruise the sagging flesh under his chin and he would fair murder Annie Laurie. 'Workers of the world unite,' he said, slumping back into the chair, 'and beware their great money trick.' Then Willie dropped his chin onto his chest and fell asleep.

Grace gave me two months' rent to pull us out of debt but I couldn't go on asking her. So I went, with my head bowed, my hands wrung together, a scarf pulled tight around my hair. I went to the social housing office. I stood in the queue. It was 1933. It was a long queue. When I got to the counter I told a man in a brown suit the Lockhart family were homeless. He said I was to speak up, he couldn't hear me. Homeless, I muttered, my cheeks ablaze. Five children, I wrote on the form. Husband – a watch-maker, I wrote but any pride I once felt for that worthy profession had gone. Age? I felt my face flush, remembering how I swallowed that lie. Johanna Lockhart – 38. William Lockhart – 59.

Three days later I went back. I stood again in the long queue. Lockhart, I enquired? Trying to smooth out the desperation lifting my voice. Excuse me! I said. Please! Have you anything for the Lockhart family? And down at the corporation housing offices there was excitement in the air. Trees and grass, they said. Running water, they said. An indoor bath, they said. And an indoor toilet! Big houses with no landlord raising the rent and banging on the ceiling. No damp either. Big windows to let the light in and good electric wiring. I couldn't believe it. Tears were running down my cheeks and for the first time in a long time it was not bitter tears. I was laughing. Yes, they said, your situation is grave enough. Five children and the head of the household with no permanent income. They waved my form in the air. It reminded me of a white flag of peace. We had gone to the top of the list. We were going to be one of the first families in a wonderful new housing scheme newly built on the outskirts of Edinburgh. They said how it was only a five mile bus run to get to the shops in town. The houses, they said, were all brand new and spanking clean. Craigmillar, that's what it was called. And we're going to have running water. And big rooms. No damp. No mice. We'll have electricity and cooking stoves. And they're putting in furniture too.

I was so happy I could have danced all the way home.

19

The Wauchope country Estate on the south east of Edinburgh was bought by the Edinburgh city corporation. Down with the slums, everyone shouted, down with half of Edinburgh's overcrowded tenements. No more poverty. No more consumption. Up with the out of town concrete purpose built large houses, and wide back greens. Down with the greedy landlords! 'Landlordism,' said Willie, 'was one of the causes of poverty. Aye,' he bawled, 'let them and their bloody rent books rot in hell. Let the corporation house its people.'

'And there'll be fresh air and green fields,' I said, wanting to skip like a bairn, 'and Edinburgh just a bus ride away.'

'It's come like I said it would,' Willie said, misty eyed, 'the revolution! Aye – we're tae lead the way intae the co-operative commonwealth!'

'Won't it be wonderful? Just wonderful.' I hadn't felt this happy for years.

'With lots of grass to play on,' said Jane, though she was hardly a child anymore.

'And a view of Arthur's Seat and a real castle,' said Jamesy.

'And we'll have a bath.' I hardly dared to believe it. 'A bath with hot running water.'

'And an indoor toilet!'

We capered around the kitchen table and when the landlady banged her broom on her ceiling for once I didn't care. We were leaving, to go to a house with an indoor toilet – and a bath!

'Good riddance to you, damned capitalist!' Willie bawled to the floor, and managed a wee jig and a twirl right there in the kitchen. Mina joined in and Jane clapped her hands. Jamesy pulled out his mouth organ and gave us a tune.

'A bath,' I kept saying, squeezing my hands together as though I was praying – 'would you credit it – a bath!'

They called Craigmillar a beacon of hope for the working classes. Houses, they said with two, even three bedrooms for the largest families. There's to be hot running water, and a back green, and spaces for the bairns to run about and play. And it's practically the countryside with green fields close by. I hadn't felt this excited since my first train journey the day I went into service.

It was a sunny day the day we flitted. The bus trundled all the way down to Portobello then climbed the long hill up to Duddingston. I could see the great gorse covered mountain of Arthur's Seat. 'Look!' Gordon shouted, his nose pressed up against the windscreen, 'the big hills. Look!' I ruffled his thick brown hair and smiled.

'We can have a picnic mother,' Donald said, 'lots of picnics!'

'Aye son. Picnics and hills, right enough.' The picturesque Loch with all its ducks and reeds came into view. The sunlight was bouncing off the water so pretty. I felt as though I could scoop it up, all that sunlight. I hummed a tune I was that glad. The bus trundled past the pretty stone houses of Duddingston village with their rose bushes, ornate iron railings and their own front doors, each painted different colours. 'Look at the pretty pots of geraniums,' I said, 'just look. We can have those too. Pink ones. And orange ones.'

'Aye mother, ye can have whatever ye like,' Willie said, and that sunny day, I believed it. The bus took forever. Chugging up Peffermill brae the craggy and ancient ruin of Craigmillar Castle came into view. There it stood, like a fairy tale castle on the brow of a hill. I lifted up my box. We were close. I knew we were close because they'd said we'd have a castle close by.

The bus screeched to a halt. 'Harewood Drive,' the conductor called out. The bus driver waited while we picked up our boxes and slung our coats over our arms. Even wee Gordon carried a box; a small one with the boot polish and a few dusters in. 'We're flitting,' I said to the conductor.

'We're going to our own house in Craigmillar.' He wished us all the best of luck, then the bus moved on and so did we.

'It's this street,' I said, shoving Gordon onto the wide stone pavement. As Gordon ran on I stared at the large block of houses ahead of me. They were heavy and big; two concrete blocks joined together. The windows were small and square and all the window frames were painted brown. All the doors were painted brown too. The concrete sparkled in the sunlight. Even though, I wished the bus hadn't gone past Duddingston village which was so pretty. These new houses in Harewood Drive would have seemed fine if the bus had brought us another way. A curtain in a house twitched as all seven of us marched, skipped and ran to our new home.

'We're not the first to move in then,' I said, nodding towards the nearby window where I could see a woman peering out at us from behind her curtain.

'One of,' said Willie, not interested in nosy neighbours. 'Right then, which house is it?'

'It's this one,' Jane said, panting under the weight of her box.

'Aye. Here's the door, faither. Here it is,' Mina called out. 'Faither should be the first one in,' she said, standing back to let her father, in his suit and bowler hat, approach the door. Number nine door opened into the stairwell and was the front door to all the houses in the block. No matter, for this occasion it was our front door. I watched Willie lower his box onto the concrete path then place both of his hands over the wooden door knob, ceremoniously. 'Oor ain place,' he said, his voice shaking with the pride and emotion of it. 'Mother. Bairns. Here it is – oor ain place.'

After we climbed the one flight of stairs we all fell silent on the landing. Even the landing was big, and clean and light filtered in from a small window on the landing. Willie nodded solemnly to the door with a large number 1 marked on the front. So this was the house we'd been allocated; block nine, house number one. Willie brought out the big iron key with a flourish. I didn't know whether to laugh or cry. Like a king before his palace Willie Lockhart placed the key in the lock.

Then we were in, running all of us. There were four rooms and not pokey wee rooms either. The bairns ran laughing from room to room. I felt this huge weight fall from me. They could run all they liked. There was no landlady with her broom. This, as Willie sang out, wis oor ain place! In the kitchen I turned the tap. Water gushed out. I ran through to the bathroom and there it was – a bath. I don't think all the riches and jewels in the world would have made me any happier. 'Bairns,' I called out, 'come and look at this – a bath!'

Before even the kist was unpacked the fiddle came out. The bairns skipped about the living room and I clapped along with the tune. I knew Willie Lockhart well enough by now. The mood for a party was on him. I glanced out of the big living room window onto the wide street below. It was beginning to get dark. Only a few lamp-posts lit up the street. It was quiet, like we were back in Haddington. There were no trams, carts or horses. No folks selling their wares on the street, no fish-wives calling, no men whistling. None of the bustle of Montague Street. In the distance I heard a fox bark. Over the spire of the church I saw the moon rise. I smiled to myself. Here we were in our own big house with no public house nearby, or none that I could see, and a church just a twenty minute walk away. I went back to the dancing, tapping my foot now in time to my husband's fiddle.

And that night anyway, Willie didn't wander off in search of comrades and whisky. He brought a bottle of stout from his pocket and toasted Craigmillar. 'Here's tae us,' he roared and tipped the brown liquid down his thrapple.

'Aye,' I said, 'here's tae us indeed,' and put a silent prayer up for God to look after us in our new home, hoping with a church so close by he'd hear us. Then I set about making the beds.

The two older boys had their own bedroom. The girls had one too. Wee Gordon came in with us because if I'm honest I was scared what might happen if I was left alone with Willie Lockhart. There I was, as my own mother counselled, lying in my bed, my face set against a bad marriage. I hoped and prayed that the beacon of Craigmillar would make it better.

At first it seemed as though my hopes would prove true. What a joy I felt seeing that steaming hot water gush from the taps and hearing the gurgling noises as the pipes brought in the water. The first bath I took that was not in a tin bath but in a proper bathroom made me feel like the Queen of Sheba herself, bathing in milk and honey. No more lugging pramfuls of washing off to the steamie either. In my own new kitchen I had hot water enough to wash all our clothes and a pulley for drying them. On good drying days I pegged the washing on the line in the back green. And the air was clean in Craigmillar, not like the town air back in soot-blackened Montague Street.

But the cloud that sat on me was never far away. There were few shops in this new housing scheme, but alas, there was a public house two streets away and a bad place it was or became soon enough when the men gathered there night after night.

For all my hot running water and space to walk about in I soon came to dread the hour when the public house would close and a knock would come to the door. 'Mrs Lockhart,' somebody would shout, 'Your man's lying drunk on the street.' I'd purse my lips, say nothing and off I would go to bring home my husband. Until the night I left him lying outside. The knock came again, harder. 'Did ye no hear me? I said yer man needs ye.'

'I heard you,' I muttered but still didn't rise to answer the door or go to drag him out of the gutter and guide him safely into his bed. After a while the neighbour gave up. I sat by the fire staring into the glowing coals. The bairns were all asleep. Or so I thought. Five minutes later Mina came through. She had a coat over her nightie.

'What about our father?' she said.

'Aye, that's what I'd like to know. What about him?'

'But, you've to go and bring him home. You have to.'

'Go back to sleep, go on. I'll get him in the morning.'

She burst into tears. 'But he'll be dead by then,' she wailed and next thing she ran to the front door, pulled it open and I heard her bare feet slapping down on the stone steps. That roused me. I'd leave Willie to wallow in his shame, but not my own daughter. So I ran after her and there I was, a woman who wanted to be proper and fine, shouting on the street. Mina was already bending over her father who looked like he was asleep on the pavement, one foot sticking out into the road.

'Get back into that house this minute,' I shouted at her, pulling her away from Willie.

'Say you'll help him home,' she cried.

'Of course I will. No go.' She went. Poor thing was only eight years old and it was after midnight. With my strong arms that had carried five bairns and thousands of buckets of coal and buckets of water I lifted up my husband and carried him home. The only comfort was that, when Willie was this drunk, he'd fall into bed, dead to the world – and sleep.

It was the nights he made it home by himself set my teeth on edge. I heard his unsteady footsteps in the dark stairwell and growled snatches of songs. I smelt the stench of cheap beer. Heard the lurch and tug at the door. Then he'd be in the house, clattering and a numb panic wrapped itself around my throat like groping hands. 'Leave the bairns,' I cried, getting up and trying to stop him from falling into the boy's room. 'The poor bairns.' I tugged his sleeve. 'Let them sleep for the love o' God.'

But a man needs his song, he tells me and he pushed me aside. My practised eye judged how drunk he was. I could tell how fast he'd fall asleep, or whether I'd have to fight off his grasping hands. Because a man needs his comfort. A man has his rights. I'd been told that often enough, and told what the duties of a wife entail. 'Damn it wumin. It's late and a man's got tae hae solace frae somewhere. If a prudish auld wife cannae gie it then his bairns can gie their ain faither a bloody song. Now get oot ma way!'

'Auld?'

'Aye you heard right. Auld!'

'I'll auld ye. It's you. You're the auld man. Auld enough to be my ain faither. Look at ye!'

'I said oot ma way or I'll go ben the kitchen and find that knife and I tell ye I'll kill ye. I will.'

In a blind flash of rage I imagined plunging that knife into him. That watch-maker's knife he had so often threatened me with. I'd swing for it. But I dug my nails into my hands and did nothing. Willie flung the bedroom door open and staggered in. I stood in the shadow by the door. Cold light from the white electric bulb in the hallway spilled into the boy's room. And suddenly the shame and wrongness of it all struck me like a slap in the face. I'd stood quiet far too long. I lunged forward and grabbed the back of Willie's jacket. 'No, you won't,' I growled, pulling him back. I sounded like an animal. I tugged him but he wanted that song. He pushed me off him and I fell to the ground. Then the fight was out of me. I stayed on my knees on the cold floor and watched while my husband hauled Donald out of bed. The poor boy was used to it. Same bairn, same song. He was only ten and it was midnight. He was probably not even asleep. I bit my lip hard to stop myself from crying. There was Willie, weeping, moaning, 'guid laddie, guid.' Wee Donald looked at me for I knew it was me he was singing to. *My bonnie dearie…*

When the song ended faither staggered out of the boy's room. I got up and ran into the bedroom. 'It's not right,' I muttered, bending over the boy to stroke his hair. 'I'm sorry, son.' I kissed wee Donald good-night. I heard clattering as Willie fell in the kitchen. 'That is no way to be a man,' I whispered. 'Don't learn from him, son. There are good men in this world, better than him. Go to sleep now, Donald.' He found my hand and squeezed it. It's that gave me the strength to go through to the kitchen, put the kettle on and make tea. Then to lie down in bed and bury my face in the pillow and fight the old drunk off when he groped at my cold flesh, slurring, 'a guid love song stirs a man.'

The handsome man who rows the boat, he's never far away. I've changed him over the years, given him more words and given our too quick love more outings. I tell him my sorrows. I have threaded silver into his black hair and painted kind lines about his eyes. He knows me, as well as I know myself. He knows my heart and that is something Willie has little interest in. I have written many letters to the man I love, some with paper and ink, and many more in my heart.

My dearest James

I dreamt you were walking towards me along the bank of the river. I told Grace my dream when she came yesterday to visit and I said to her it proves you are living still and she said, tosh, it is more likely the opposite for don't the dead walk in the corridors of dreams? But what does Grace know?

We have flitted again and at least from this kitchen window I can see the yellow gorse blazing on Arthur's Seat. And there are birds here a plenty and not just pigeons and starlings but blackbirds and I have seen ducks and swans fly overhead. Here the buildings are squat and drab but there is beauty close by. If I had the time I could walk to Duddingston Loch and see bulrushes and swaying reeds. Some people skate there in the winter. It takes an hour to walk there from here. I did go once with the bairns but no sooner was I there than it was time to turn back. I am always working, it seems. I read in the newspaper of a condition they call shell-shock. It said a soldier returned just last month to his home in Renfrew, right glad, so he said, that the war was over. No, they told him, it is 1933. The war ended in 1918. He had lost fifteen years and of course his family hardly knew him and he didn't know them.

But I would know you. If you came back from wandering and called my name I swear I would leave this no good husband of mine and run into your arms. Baxter has put into my head that you did not die with the regiment, but have shell-shock. She says the tea-leaves tell her you are living still. She says she will try and find you. Grace and Baxter are like two opposites of the see-saw of my heart. Grace says I must forget you and make the most of what I have. Baxter says there is magic in the world and miracles happen more often than we think, and I should hope that we can still be together.

I am forever yours

God protect you and bring you home

Johanna

20

It was not long after we arrived in Craigmillar that the wonderful parcels from America started to arrive. 'Och, would you take a look at that,' said Willie, holding the brown paper parcel up on high, examining it, then with great pomp untying the string. 'Comics frae auntie Faith,' he announced.

'You're a dark horse, Willie Lockhart,' I said, in a good mood with the bairns skipping about the room. 'I thought Clara was your only sister.'

Willie shook his head and flung his arm to the west, pointing to America. 'This one's a distant cousin, more like,' he said, 'wi no bairns of her ain.' For a moment he looked fit to burst into tears. 'So she's got a wee soft spot for mine.' Then he snatched up a comic and roared, like one of the characters I suppose.

I folded my arms over my pinny, and smiled. I was glad for cousin Faith, way over in the New World, with no bairns of her own. Once every couple of months the comics came and even Christmas couldn't have been better. Coloured comics with pictures and stories and sometimes a wee tin car or wind-up toy nestled in among the rolled up comics. Good old auntie Faith, the bairns yelled, fighting over who would get the comics and me saying I'd send them right back over the Atlantic ocean to America if they didn't wheesht and behave.

The bairns all went to the new school and the stories they brought home at dinner time would have broken a mother's heart. How hardly any bairns in Craigmillar wore shoes, half of them fell asleep at their desks and a good few had shaved heads. It put me in mind of Geordie MacPhee, and a slobbery red gobstopper. 'Wee Malcolm's got bandy legs,' Jamesy told us, as we all sat round the kitchen table, tucking in to mashed potatoes and a thin mince.

'It's oranges wee Malcolm needs,' I said, then the bairns all started asking for a bite of an orange.

'If you're very lucky you might find one in your stocking at Christmas,' I told them. 'Just think yourself fortunate you're eating at all.' We ate in silence after that, me wondering if I might beg an extra shilling from Willie that night to go and buy some oranges, scared that my own children might get bandy legs and scurvy.

'Wit's wrong wi brambles,' Willie said, when I told him how I was worried the bairns might get ill.

'It's November,' I reminded him, 'the brambles have gone.'

During the day Willie went round the houses, knocking on doors and asking if anybody needed a clock or a watch mended. I helped him set up a table in the corner of the sitting room. I could well remember life without electricity but so quickly we couldn't imagine living without it. Willie had a small light bulb to work by at that table. But there was precious little work. It was 1935 and half the men in Craigmillar were out of work. So Willie returned from his door to door rounds with an old clock or a cheap watch to mend, if he was lucky. 'They're a right poor lot in this place,' he said, tipping his palms out to show me his meagre finds, like a proud salmon fisherman who comes home with a minnow. 'What a man needs is his ain shop.'

I laughed as though he had asked for an ermine frock coat and a motor car, but later, watching him bent over his small fry and seeing his long slim fingers nimble at such intricate work I grasped at a thread of hope. Maybe a shop would be the making of him? For all his drinking and sorry states he managed, God knows how, to rise early, splash cold water on his face and put his suit on, plus pocket watch and bowler hat, looking, and I smiled remembering mother's word – respectable.

So I scoured the newspaper and eventually found a small shop to let. It was in Newington, not a stone's throw from Montague Street as it happened, and the monthly rent, like the shop, was small. Surely Willie could manage that? I put on my dark blue church coat. I put a cloche hat on, pulled down to half cover my face. I gazed at my reflection in the mirror then quickly looked away. 'You ready then faither,' I called, pulling my gloves on.

'Aye mother, all ready and correct.' I glanced at him, this small squat man with his thumbs hooked into his waistcoat pockets and his shoes gleaming. His hair was turning white. 'Mr Lockhart the watch-maker is ready for his shop.' He winked at me and I laughed. 'And while we're at it – why don't we make a day o' it in Edinburgh toon?' He jangled a few coins. I glanced back into the kitchen. The washing was done. The bairns were all at school. The ironing was done. And we could have chips for tea.

'Well,' said I, 'let's see about the shop first.'

There was a nip to the wind but enough blue in the sky to, so Willie said, make a pair of sailor's trousers, and on that bus going into town I swear I couldn't keep the smile off my face.

'Well faither. The paper said it was small.'

'Guid thing a watch is a wee enough thing.'

We stood on the pavement in front of the shop. Its proportions put me in mind of a doll's house. 'Aye faither, but if business goes well, ye could always find a bigger shop.'

The newspaper had exaggerated saying the shop was small. Miniscule would have been more fitting. The shop was squeezed in between two other shops at St. Leonard's, as though the baker shop on one side and the engravers on the other each sold off, in hard times, a few inches of their shop to make another. But there was something cosy and dwarf like about that tiny shop and I thought it would suit Willie Lockhart just fine. So the deal was done and after the handshake and the signing of his name my husband seemed to grow and swell. I felt happy for him. I could see it mattered. A man like Willie needed his own shop.

'Guid things come to those who wait,' he said, turning to me once the transactions were complete. Beaming from ear to ear he kissed me on the cheek. 'I am my ain man at long last.'

21

People thought we were rich! I was a good house-keeper. I had been well trained and knew a good many ways to remove stains, thin stews, darn old socks, mend shoes, turn thread-bare towels into dusters, use left-overs, scrub faces, wash and brush hair, turn hems and make clothes. And – on top of all this I did a bit of mending for the minister and two of the church elders. It was Jane at the Sunday school who told them what a dab hand I was with the sewing needle. I didn't tell Willie and with him out the house most evenings it was easy enough to conceal the mending work. I kept the few pennies I made in a jar at the back of the cupboard. More than once we would have gone hungry without those few coppers.

'Ye hang out a lovely washing, Mrs Lockhart, I'll say that for you,' Mrs Mather next door said. I told her how to keep her whites white. Many's the day, with the first spits of rain, I brought her washing in for her. I gave her recipes for shortbread and girdle scones and when I made ginger biscuits I always put a few through for her. Even though, her bairns still looked ragged and hungry. More times than I could count one of them came in, stared wide-eyed at my good clean white table-cloth as though they'd never seen a table far less a cloth upon it, then asked for something to eat.

The myth of the well-to-do Lockhart family was kept alive by my good house-keeping and the once a month parcel from America. There was a scramble to see who would get to it first then the boys ran around the house shouting at the top of their voices, 'it's from auntie Faith, auntie Faith, we've got new comics from auntie Faith!'

I imagined the never-clapped-eyes-upon Auntie Faith; the great comic benefactor, as sitting in a rocking chair in a clapboard house and speaking in a funny accent. I imagined she had taken a boat from Glasgow in her youth and headed for the New World. I imagined she was rich.

Out of that monthly brown paper parcel with its fancy stamps came one-legged pirates braving stormy seas to capture ships and grow rich on its booty, swaggering cowboys riding bare-back on white Palomino horses, lassoing screaming red Indians who wore fine feather head-dresses and moon-eyed, jaw dropping expressions. There were monsters tall as mountains with hairy bodies and crunching house-squashing steps, helpless pale maidens leaning from burning castles, screaming to be saved, their long white arms reaching towards broad-shouldered heroes wearing black hats and thick belts who slashed through bushes and stabbed snakes. These swooning heroes had little balloons above their brave faces with words like – **never fear**, or **jump into my arms!** There would usually be a blind-folded captain, forced to walk the plank by the desperado pirates who had taken over his ship. Would he find a last minute means of escape? Would the deaf and dumb cabin boy, tied up in the ship's hold, save the day? Would the ghost rattling around in the haunted house scare off the prospective buyers? Find out next month girls and boys.

I know because they told me all about it. They acted it out. Over and over.

'This is even better than The Broons,' wee Gordon shouted.

'And better than Oor Wullie,' shouted Jamesy.

'Aye well, aren't ye all lucky to have an auntie Faith in America?' said Faither, not above having a keek at the comics himself.

'Oh aye,' they all shouted, 'guid old Auntie Faith!'

Grace liked to read the comics. She visited, coming over on the bus when she could make it, and she fair cheered up my day. And I needed somebody to tell my troubles to. 'In the police cell, drunk – a whole night. Would you credit the shame of it,' I told her, my voice hushed. 'I sent Jamesy to bring him home the next morning. Don't get them putting father's name in the paper, I told him. It was awful, Grace, just awful! He was dishevelled, like a tramp.' Grace sighed and shook her head. She had little time for Willie Lockhart, and wasn't shy to say so. That wasn't the first time she counselled me to up and go.

'Easy enough to say,' I said, bustling with the tray I'd set out for us. Just then wee Gordon came running through and jumped up onto her lap. I swear the way she cuddled wee Gordon you'd think the breath would go out of him. 'Do you not miss it?' I said later when we were in the living room sipping our tea. I had made a current loaf specially.

'Miss what?' she said. 'Being in service?' Our days in-service was our favourite topic.

I shook my head and smiled. 'No. Having bairns of your own. Being a mother.'

Her face darkened. 'Not after what happened to Sadie. I vowed then Johanna, no man would ever trap me, and I've kept to it. And anyway,' she brightened up, 'you've got plenty. I'm very happy to spoil wee Gordon once a fortnight. I don't need more than that.'

We both fell silent then. Any mention of Sadie always had that effect. It brought a gloom into the room. I tried not to think of the poor girl, swinging from a rope, her belly swollen, her face turning blue. I tried to think of Auntie Faith's comics and the fifty-foot woman from the Amazon jungle ripping trees out by their roots.

'That's a lovely moist current loaf anyway, Johanna.'

It was, but I didn't have the stomach for it anymore.

'They're saying the wee yin's a guid pupil at the school,' mother tells father one night.

They're both sitting in front of the fire drinking beer. Father's got his boots off and I can see the steam rise from his socks, and smell them too, sour and vinegary, 'Aye, a right guid wee worker.' I'm up at the table with Jemima, shelling peas, listening, the door ajar between us.

'That's coz she's a Blackie,' answers he, all laughing and proud. 'Guid worker's in wir blood.' Sometimes when they argue they pit the Scott bairns up against the Blackie bairns. The best thing in the world, it seems, is to be a good worker, and father was always on about what braw workers the Blackies were, no like the Scott bairns, wee shirkers the lot of them and what about that Martha that can't even make her man a pan of stew.

'Shut yer face man,' says mother, 'and stop trying tae pit yersel in the picture. Johanna – yer wee lassie – oor wee lassie, is guid at the school. School work I'm on aboot. And Martha does her best, ye ken that.'

'Aye weel, guid fir her, as long as I dinnae huv tae eat her best. And guid fir the bairn. Guid fir you JoHann.'

But mother isn't done. 'And that teacher, right fancy pants Miss Macdonald, says she could go on tae the college and be a teacher.'

'Jane Scott, get it intae yer skull, Blackie's are workers. Honest hard workers. The likes o' us dinnae go tae 'the college' and dinnae go pittin' fancy ideas in her heid. Just gie's her that bit further tae fall.'

'But I would like to be a teacher,' I call out, my voice a bit too posh and a bit too like Miss Macdonald's.

Then I hear the wooden legs of his chair scrape across the floor. I hear father make a snorting noise. I hear him march through to the kitchen in his damp stocking soles. He's got a piece of coal in his hand. He's waving it in front of my face. 'We work wi' oor hands hen,' he says slowly, cupping my chin in one dirty hand and glaring at me. Horrified I watch the piece of coal loom down on me. I try to squirm away but he holds me tight. 'And Blackies get dirty.' I smell the coal. The sooty smell clings to my throat. The black craggy thing looms closer. I feel it press onto my nose. He scrapes the coal across my cheek as though it's chalk and I'm a black-board. 'And we dinnae get above oor sels.'

I whimper. Jemima gasps. He pushes me down on the table then draws the coal across my forehead. It hurts the way he presses the coal over my face. Jemima just sits there staring and the peas all roll onto the floor. 'An when we pit oor heids on the bed tae sleep at night it's coz we've done a honest day's work.' By this time my face is all black and I'm crying. 'Aye work!' He's shouting now, his face all red and twisted. 'Wi' yer hands! Till yer bones near break and yer back's that bent. Work! That's yer lot, wi' never an end to it, d'ye hear me?'

'Leave the bairn alone,' mother shouts but she doesn't come through to me. She's tired, I can hear it in her voice. 'Leave the bloody wee worker alone.'

I am nine years old. I know I'll never be a teacher. Father goes out, once he's done, and he slams the door. The house shakes. I hear his steps on the stairs.

Jemima runs through to the room, crying to mother. I sit up and shudder. I put my hands to my face then look at them – they're black. The lines are all black. Tears make the coal dust stick to me. Work – that's what I see – years and years of it and no long dress going swish-swish, swish-swish.

Mother comes through and cleans me up while Jemima, sobbing, picks the peas off the floor. Mother's mouth is tight closed and her jaw set.

'Aye, that's aboot the sum o' it,' she says, rubbing my face hard with a damp rag. 'And ye canny blame the man. He's oot here at six, rain, hail or shine – tae put shoes on yer feet and breid in yer belly. Ye canny blame him hen. That fancy teacher wifie – wit does she ken? That's no real work. She'll teach ye letters and stuff, but it's yer ain folk teach ye what life's really like.'

The gas mantle flickers and a greenish light falls on the side of mother's face. Around her mouth lines eat into her skin. 'Aye,' I say, fighting back the tears and the childish dreams. 'Aye mother.'

I work harder after my face was blackened. When father comes home from work I make sure I'm always busy doing something and as soon as he takes off his tackety smelly boots I make a great show of lifting them and putting them on newspaper. Then I scrub all the dirt off them then rub dubbing on. And I sing as I work, so he can see how happy I am in my work.

Have you ever, ever, ever
In your long legged life
Seen a long legged sailor
With a short legged wife…

I still love the school, but it's different now. I won't be a teacher. Miss Macdonald tells us about Black Sambo sitting under a palm tree in the sun, his face all sooty. I feel very sorry for little Black Sambo. Miss Macdonald says he's a black man from Africa. After that lesson they all call me Black Sambo but Miss Macdonald tells them to wash their mouths out with carbolic soap.

'There are many black people in the world,' she says, 'and they are good people. God,' she says, 'made people in different colours which is to do with the sun and never forget we are all made in His image. In Scotland we don't get that much hot sun so we're quite peely-wally. And,' she says, 'foreign people don't all speak the same as us. Repeat after me children – bon jour. You never know when that might come in handy.'

So all forty of us, sitting up straight on our low benches, shout out in our sing-song voices – bon jour!

22

Though it was the decade of the great economic slump things had never been better for the Lockhart family. The shop was managing to pay the rent, give Willie a good conceit of himself and though my pay-packet was little to sing about, I managed to put food on the table and clothes on the children's backs. I was still bringing in some extra coppers from my mending, but could feel the strain of it on my eyes. Some nights, when Jamesy and Donald went off to the Scout group in the church hall Jane and Mina helped me with the mending.

And when Willie did come home drunk, and I can't pretend these days were behind us, I only had to remind myself of my hot running water, indoor toilet and bath, then even the bleakest of days had a sparkle to them. I sang in my work and the children were a great help to me. Children? They were taller than me and looking more like young men and women every day. It'll be grand-children next, I thought. Jane was already fourteen. She wanted to stay on at the school then go to the university. The teacher said she was bright enough. Of course Willie put his foot down. She was to leave school and find a job and bring home a few pennies to pay for her keep. She didn't argue. She knew nobody from Craigmillar went to the university. 'I'll find a job in an office, mother,' she said. She put a brave face on it but couldn't hide the disappointment in her voice. 'I'll be a help to you.'

'Aye, Jane,' I said, 'you're a good wee worker.' I was the echo of my own mother's voice. Aye, we were all good wee workers.

There is a shoe shop in Leith Walk with an advertisement for an assistant posted in the shop window.

It's the day of my fourteenth birthday and mother goes into the dowdy leather smelling shop with me standing behind her, all scrubbed clean with my best skirt on and white blouse. I stand there smiling like she told me to while she speaks to the manageress. I smile so much my cheeks hurt and I feel like I'm going to be sick. It's the smell – leather like twenty dead cows in a slaughterhouse. The manageress, with her thin blue lips, stares at me, her beady little eyes checking, so I guess anyway, for lice. It's been a while since these black beasties have lived in my head but now, still smiling, I start to scratch. I can't help it.

'She's not got nits I hope?' I hear the shop lady ask. But Jane Scott can give as good as she gets. She might be a poor woman living in a room and kitchen in Leith, married to a man she has tae hide money from and haul out the public house, but she can stand up for herself.

'Not a bit o' it. She's clean through and through. And a great worker,' she adds, glaring at me. I stop scratching. And start the next day.

It's not the work itself I like. The best part is going to work. It feels as though I am part of the great Scottish work force and there we all are, nodding to each other, hailing each other 'good morning' or 'good evening' and all of us doing our bit. Only, selling shoes doesn't seem important. I imagine what it would be like if I just keep on walking, past the shoe shop, up Leith Walk and onto Princes Street then maybe onto a train. Because it doesn't take much looking to see there's more world than your own wee house, more streets than Gordon Street, more to the world than Leith.

As well as the horse-drawn carts clanking and rolling over the cobbled roadways there are a few motor cars. They have loud horns and handle-bar moustachioed drivers and you have to scoot off the road quick if they start their tooting. And when you walk on the road you have to lift your skirt and petticoat because the last thing you want is horse-dung on your hems.

***

'How is business faither?' I asked when he came home in the early evening in time to carry the soup to the table.

'Business is grand missus, just grand. You ken of course my shop is close tae the university. I'm getting tae know medical students. Now they've got fancy watches – and of course they need tae know what time it is. Oh aye, many's the socialist debate take's place in my wee shop.'

I didn't doubt it. 'Plenty work then?'

'Well ye ken, it takes time – tae get established. But I am getting myself established.' He sprinkled curry powder on his soup and shlurped loudly.

I well imagined how Willie Lockhart would go about getting himself established. A few poems no doubt. The fiddle too would get an airing. The Ragged Trousered Philanthropists, quoted to whoever would listen. The 'system' blamed and cursed till the air turned blue then a dram to seal every deal.

'Women don't understand business,' he said when I complained about the paltry pay packet and how could a family of seven cope on a few shillings? Then he told me how business is a slow mistress you need to woo in different ways. 'It's no just about making money,' he said, 'och no, the day we work purely for money we're guid as dead.' He speared a dough-ball, mopped it in gravy and ate it. 'And don't forget it bairns,' said he, chomping and swinging his fork back and forth like a pendulum.

'Aye, an with'oot it we're good as dead too.'

'Wheesht woman. Yer spirit's no dead. The rank is but the guinea's stamp missus, the man's the gowd for a' that!'

I shook my head, gathered up the dirty plates and cutlery then dished out the semolina, in time to his; 'What tho' on hamely fare we dine!' There was no arguing with Rabbie Burns.

After dinner, if the mood was on him, he'd go over and lift up the window in the sitting room and stand there playing his fiddle. His audience gathered from up and down Harewood Drive. Sometimes son Jamesy took out his moothie and joined in and so the two of them, father and son, regaled their comrades in Craigmillar. Sometimes it was the old Scot's tunes, but more often these days it was the modern tunes:

Grab your coat and get your hat
Leave your worries on the doorstep
Life can be so sweet
On the sunny side of the street.

I liked that song. I took wee Gordon up in my arms and birled him around. Round and round till the room was spinning and he was squealing in delight.

If I never had a cent
I'd be rich as Rockefeller
Gold dust at my feet
On the sunny side of the street.

The older ones capered about the floor, chanting how they could, 'dance like the Americans.' Donald swung me round. 'Dance wi' me mother,' he said, 'put wee Gordon down and come and dance like Auntie Faith.'

'Now just you wait laddie.' I put Gordon on the floor under the table so he wouldn't get trodden on, 'and I'll show ye how tae waltz.' Outside on the street the crowd gathered under our window were singing along, as though they were serenading us, and there was I, waltzing with my ten year old son in the sitting room.

'Where did ye learn to waltz mother?' Donald said, proving himself a capable dancer the way his palm pressed gently against the small of my back. It wouldn't be long before girls a lot younger than his mother would be waltzing in his arms.

After the church us servants are free for four hours, to write letters in our rooms, or take the fresh air.

Sadie's a scullery maid. She's from Leith too. She links her arm in mine after church and off we go, like two sisters, to take the autumn Perthshire air.

'Don't ye cry for yer mother and father?' she asks me, when we're out on the country lane. Sadie snaps off pink dog roses and we wear them in our hair.

'No,' I tell her, remembering that thin and shabby looking man that had waved to her all these months ago at Waverly station. 'Do you?'

'Oh aye. Every night. And the stable boy is always pulling faces at me. And cook gie's me the tiniest plate o' gristly mince. I tell you Johanna, it's gravy, it's no mince.'

'Oh, you poor thing, well, ye'll never guess what I did – the very first day. I tried to cut the beef. It was that tough I couldn't manage. It flew across the room.'

'Never?'

'Aye, really, and it landed in the butler's beer!'

'Oh Johanna. Ye must have howled. Did ye no cry fir yer mother and father then?'

'No – Lizzie says we all make mistakes. And everybody laughed.'

We carry on chatting and taking the Comrie air. We pick violets for our button holes then play tig and suddenly we're bairns again. Then just as quickly young ladies. 'Of course you'll need to know a waltz, Johanna,' she says to me gravely. 'If you want a click ye need to know about dancing.' I giggle. 'Here, it's like this,' says Sadie, putting her hand round my waist and pulling me along, 'look, one and two then stop.' Seeing she's serious I try. I stand on her feet. I laugh till I cry but she keeps on. 'Johanna, you have to learn. How will ye get a husband if ye cannae dance?'

So down by the river in Comrie in the early Springtime we waltz, hidden by cherry trees in blossom so we won't be seen by passers-by. Then, when I can't concentrate on the steps anymore we dander along by the side of the river. We toss our by now wilted dog roses into the river, making wishes. 'I wished for to be a fine lady,' Sadie said, 'married to a rich man.' She lifted her skirt and birled, laughing at the thought. 'And you Johanna?'

'Love,' I answer her, shyly, watching the pink flower float away on the water. 'That would be enough for me. To find a good loving man to marry me.'

For a long time we throw stones into the water then link arms, skip along the bank and before long the two of us are singing away at the top of our voices; *all things bright and beautiful, all creatures great and small, all things wise and wonderful, the Lord God made them all*; and a hop, a skip and a giggle in the sunlight.

When we part that afternoon we both have wide smiles on our faces. What a grand thing to have a friend. We keep turning back to wave to each other, while she walks to Cuthie Bank which sits at the foot of a craggy hill and me down the green and white sweet smelling valley to Grange House. It takes a good hour to walk back and many a hymn to give a spring to the stepping, or the waltzing – one two, one two three. Who will I marry…wait and see!

***

I nodded at my son. 'A friend I once had in service. Sadie – bless her soul, Sadie was her name. Sadie Macdonald. She taught me.' I pictured Sadie young and alive. I pictured her laughing, and dancing. I tossed back my head, as if I was fifteen again. 'So if I was ever asked I'd know what to do.'

'And were ye mother? Were ye ever asked?'

'Yer asking me, aren't you, Donald? And just look at us, a right pair o' eejits.'

'No, we're not,' he said, whirling me around and laughing. 'You are beautiful mother – beautiful.'

23

I don't like the shoe shop.

School made the world seem a big place. In the shop the world shrinks till I feel like tiny Alice in Wonderland and suddenly – puff! – all that learning – gone for ever!

'Miss Blackie. Fit Bertie Macduff wi' stout boots and be quick about it.'

'Do I . . . have to?'

Miss Chapman looks ready to slap me one, but my fear of Bertie Macduff is greater than my fear of Miss Chapman. He sometimes follows me about the streets and makes schlurping wet kissing noises behind my back. He works in the roperie in Leith and has thick blubbery lips that hang down and his mouth is always a bit open. Mother says people who can't breathe through their nose do that, and she says there's a lot in the roperie like that, but it makes him look gormless and horrible.

'Aye, you do. Just ignore any cheek he gives ye. Now go on, serve him.'

'Thon's a bonny wee face – a right bonnie wee face,' Bertie sings, the reek of beer mixed with all the other reeks. He doesn't even have socks on. His manky bare foot slaps down into my cupped hands in time to his song. I can't stand the feel of his sweaty, hairy foot. It's disgusting. I drop his foot and run up to Miss Chapman, crying.

'Do I have to? Do I really have to serve him Miss Chapman? I cannae abide him. And the way he stares at me. And he stinks.'

'Customer's a customer,' Miss Chapman hisses through pursed lips. She stands at the counter with her elbows flung out, her hands clenched on her hips. She has her back turned on Bertie Macduff. 'He's paying yer wages and if he gives you cheek just do what Jesus did.'

'Wit was that, Miss Chapman?' I say, sniffling and blowing my nose, 'wit was it Jesus did?'

'He turned the other cheek Blackie, he turned the other cheek.'

***

I wasn't yet forty but I felt old. The afternoons were worst. Not that I had the liberty to sit idle and day-dream but whether it was scrubbing the floor, bringing in the washing, chopping the potatoes, rolling pastry, mending clothes, the thoughts crept in unbidden. I tried to push them away. I prayed and sang hymns, but the thoughts found their way in anyway, in between making the bed and pegging a sheet on the line. How it all could have been so different. How I could have made wiser choices; how I could have married a decent man; a man like James Melville. How Willie's drinking was somehow my fault. How I wasn't good enough, or gentle enough, or warm enough. How I was lacking in my duty as a wife. How it was my flaws that drove him into the public house.

Maybe it *was* my fault. I was hardly a wife in that sense any more. I couldn't stand his hands on me. I couldn't abide the reek of beer that came from him, and the language when he was drunk. I couldn't stand the sight of my own husband lying in the gutter and the smell of him when I draped his limp arm around my shoulder and carried him home. I was repulsed. He was beginning to look haggard. He had a lump on his neck. He said it was from playing the fiddle. I kept telling him to get it seen to but he wouldn't hear of it. And his threats of stabbing hardly melted my heart towards him. It's your duty, that's what he was forever telling me, slurring the words, pawing at my body and me thinking, dear God in heaven, what kind of duty is this? 'And your duty, husband,' I said, pushing him off me, 'what of your duty? Me penniless because of your drinking – your own bairns in patched up second hand clothes, is this what you call duty?'

'It's the damned system, woman.' His answer for everything.

The more he drank and shamed us, the more I scrubbed the house, made and mended the bairns' clothes, fed them as best as I could manage and trimmed their hair. I was forever taking down hems, turning one thing into something else. A pillow case that had started out as a blouse. A liberty bodice that had been a dress. We had a white tablecloth on the table and in the spring I gathered daffodils and put them in a jar on the table. My children never went bare-footed and lice didn't last long under my bone comb. 'Folks think we're rich mother,' Gordon said.

I wondered what else folks thought. 'Maybe we are,' I said. 'We've got our health and a good house. You go to the school, and the Boy's club, and the Sunday school, and isn't that the sun shining outside? Aye, maybe we are rich.'

Gordon rubbed his stomach and his little round face beamed up at me. 'Sponge and custard today,' he said, drooling at the mouth, 'my favourite!'

I shooed him away from under my feet. I had to make it first. And the sausage meat and onions before any pudding ever graced the table.

24

Once every season there was a family social on in the church hall where someone would play the piano and we'd have a bit of a sing-song. Sometimes Jemima took the bus over from her house in Granton to join us. Poor Jemima didn't hear too well and she would sit there with her hand to her ear, telling people to 'speak up,' when they stood to recite a poem or a piece of prose. Some of these nights you'd even see folks up treading the boards with a Gay Gordons or an Eightsome Reel. I would hum along and tap my feet. 'It's grand to get out, isn't it mother?' Donald would say, breathless after a good old stomp about the hall.

'Aye, it is that son,' I said, glad for him, glad for the children, relieved if their father sat quiet enough, and with the minster's eyes on him he usually did, but afterwards always said how he couldn't abide these po-faced affairs with their weak tea, thin sandwiches and old piano that needed tuning. He seldom lasted out the whole evening, and I wasn't sorry to see him don his hat and slip out the back door. I breathed easier with him gone.

For weeks the bairns would go on about these church socials, going over the songs we sung and the turns that folks did. I was pleased to see them happy, but it was the dress-making evening class that was my highlight.

The corporation had started up evening classes to boost morale and get people learning new things. I took Mina and Gordon with me, along to the class at Niddrie Marischal. Mina and Gordon usually sat in the corner and got on with drawing and pouring over their comics. It was Jane talked me into going along to this evening class, saying how it would get me out and meeting people. And she was right. I loved it.

The sewing teacher, Miss Strachan, wore odd-looking clothes she had made and she looked a bit of a sight but she was a fine enough teacher. Poor woman had half a finger missing. 'Want to know what happens when you put your finger too close to the needle in the sewing machine?' she often said. Then, as though she was a magician pulling a white rabbit from a top hat she stuck up her half finger. 'Ha-ha! That's what happens!'

After a few weeks Miss Strachan hailed me as her star pupil. I blushed and shook my head. Mina wanted me to make dresses like the film star Judy Garland wore and kept pushing patterns from Vogue and Ladies Fashion Weekly under my nose but I kept my hands busy with aprons and nightshirts, not heeding fads. This evening I was working on an A line skirt for Jane and was pleased with the shape of it. Good tight stitching and a nice strong woollen material. She was hoping for a job in an office and I wanted her to look smart. Plus it would keep her warm in the winter.

We were walking back through Niddrie and I was talking away, about how I would need to keep an eye out for a new thimble. I was that excited with the evening class and the progress I'd made with the skirt, and of course it was great to get out and have a good natter with the other women. It reminded me of the old days in the steamie. Now there was a proper natter. So I was in fine spirits that night and even the drab stretches of grey concrete and swirls of litter didn't get me down the way they sometimes did.

'It's no good trying to push a needle through a thick bit o' material if you don't have a proper strong thimble,' I said to my daughter. Gordon wasn't interested in dress-making. He was busy being an American pirate and acting like he was climbing the rigging.

Mina was only half listening. I didn't care. I enjoyed nattering. We hurried home, past men sitting on stone steps smoking Capstan cigarettes, past women trudging home with prams piled high with messages and three or four straggling bairns at their feet.

Someone shouted out, 'got a spare copper?' I fumbled in my pocket and gave him a ha'penny. Poor soul, another tramp, another of these ragged men begging for bread. The mile-post inspectors, we called them.

'God keep you,' he called after me. Then I carried on, back to my stories of what I would make next and who I would make it for. And there was Donald needing a new waistcoat and I said maybe for his next birthday he might be lucky. And all the way down Harewood Drive we discussed the colour of it. Would it be navy or beige or maroon? And would we be home before our Boy Scouts, Jamesy and Donald got in, I wondered.

Before I opened the front door I knew something was wrong. We were in the stair when the reek of gas caught at my throat. I gasped, hurried ahead and pushed the front door open.

Willie was slumped over the gas cooker, drunk but still standing, just. Gas hissed out and God knows how long it had been slowly hissing out into the kitchen. A slop of porridge oats made a trail over the linoleum from the pantry to the cooker. 'Sshbloody pan,' he slurred. He looked up and swayed. His hand grasped the black iron ring on the cooker.

I dropped my bag of sewing things on the floor. 'For God's sake!' I shouted, coughing and choking. Mina and Gordon were right behind me. I clamped my hand over my mouth and waved them back. 'Get through to your bed,' I shouted. I heard them both whimper and scream as I lunged towards the cooker. I panicked, wondering where Jane was then remembered she was staying with a friend overnight. Choking I turned the gas knob off then dashed over to the window. I pulled back the curtains and yanked the window up. The fresh cold air hit me. I gasped like someone half drowned then swung round to see Willie loosen his grip on the iron ring and slump slowly to the ground. Even in the midst of all that panic I thought how he looked like a thick lumpy bread sauce being poured onto a plate. But now he was face down on the oat strewn floor and groaning. 'Bloody noshin fir a hard worhin man tae eat. Noshin!' He was rolling about, trying to heave himself up onto his elbows and every time slumping back down.

Watching him, still choked with the fumes, I felt a red anger boil inside me. I glared down at this pitiful sight of a husband. I married this man. I bore him five bairns and here he was, drunken sod, sprawled out amongst the porridge oats and shouting how there was nothing to eat and his children witnessing the whole sorry fiasco.

'I could have married a decent man,' I shouted, glowering over him. 'I could have had a proper good man!' I wanted to kick him. I wanted to drag him by the shirt tails into the street, just like the many times I had been dragged out into the night to lift him up and carry him home. I couldn't take it anymore. Him drunk and swearing. Him lying next to me in bed. His promises and lies. I wanted to drag him out onto the street and leave him there. Let it rain. Let the neighbours stare. Let him freeze to death.

'Why dishn't you?' he slurred. His words were like a slap across the face. Even pissed as a lord he knew he'd got me. So he said it again, lying there on the floor, porridge oats all over him, 'why didn't you? Cosh he didnae want ye. Yer fancy man didnae want ye. Jist like yer ain mither didnae want ye.'

'You lied to me, Willie Lockhart,' I shouted, sobbing now. 'You lied about your age. You lied about being a tee-totaller. Did you lie about being a soldier as well? You never did fight in the Great War, did ye? Others did. Oh aye, others lost their life fighting for us. Brave young soldiers died for us. Honest good men. Decent men. But you? You were too old. What else have you lied about? Tell me?'

'He didnae want ye, did he? Naebody else would have ye.'

'Stop it,' I shouted. 'Stop it. You lied to me.'

'I didnae lie,' he said, his voice fat and wet. I saw tears course down his blubbering face and heard them splat onto the floor.

I looked at the trail of porridge oats on the floor and thought of the story of Hansel and Gretel and how Hansel made a trail of bread crumbs through the forest to find his way home and how the birds ate them. The house and its walls and stench of gas fell open inside me, like a slowly collapsing house made of bread.

Before the walls tumble I see the pictures, the flickering candle light. I can hear the games in the street, the songs chanting like innocent ghosts, the pictures dancing on the wall, and there's Sadie running in a hay field with a garland of ivy twisted in her long dark hair, and brother Jimmy, laughing at the way his little sister's body bends and squashes up in the hall of mirrors, and us bairns are leaping over the lapping waves of Portobello. Even the grand house in Perthshire is there with its rare smell of game and roses. And Baxter, still sewing that never-ending quilt and telling her jokes. Mr Moody's bear is performing still, smashing apples. There's my own father dancing in the street with a carnation in his button-hole and James Melville is there, rowing, forever rowing, with the lazy sound of water slapping against the hull of his boat but his boat is slowly sinking and as his boat goes under red poppies spring up and float upon the water. And there is young Johanna, on a bench in a woodland setting, with a letter held in her hand.

Imagine a letter, the man in a black frock coat says, to a young girl with her life spread out before her, imagine a love letter. Then a blinding light flashes.

The walls fall. There never was a love letter. Though how I wished to God there was. Yes I had written letters. But where would I send them? I knew how to form my letters. I could shape the letter J beautifully. Tears stung my eyes. **Dear James, I love you, Johanna.**

I followed the trail of oats back to my husband's arm and his shuddering body, him all dressed in his best and filthy with it. I saw stains of beer down his front. I saw the way his tie was pulled over to the side as though someone had yanked it in a fight. I saw the cleaning and washing I'd have to do.

'You lied,' I said, quieter now.

He coughed. 'I thought you woudnae gie an auld man a chance.' He was whimpering now like a dog. 'Ye're a guid women mosher,' he sniffed, running his sleeve over his snotty nose and tear-stained face. 'Dish I tell ye shat?'

'Ye could have had us a' dead.' I bent down and grabbed his boots and dragged him through to the bathroom. His head bumped on the cold floor. His arm hit against the table leg. He yelped and whimpered. I didn't care. I had been far too good to Willie Lockhart.

'I'm awfy shorry, mother. Shorry. I wish hungry.'

'Wheesht man,' I snapped, dropping his ankles and letting him slump down on the floor next to the bath. He was filthy. 'The toilet's the right place for you.'

I heard the front door open. I heard my brave Boy Scouts gasp and cough. I heard them run through the house. 'Mother, what's the matter? Mother?' I heard their urgent footsteps behind me. 'Mother, in the name of God, what happened?' I didn't answer. My husband lay sprawled out on the bathroom floor in front of me. I couldn't bear to turn round and look at my sons. 'What a disgrace.' That was Donald. I could hear the disgust in his voice. The repulsion. 'For God's sake faither,' I heard Jamesy cry at my back, 'you should be ashamed of yourself.'

Still I couldn't face them. Without turning round I said, 'don't speak to your father like that.'

'But for heaven's sake, mother, he's…he's…drunk…and…'

'He's your father.' I stared down at him, as disgusted as they were. 'And aye, he's drunk.' I left him lying there and backed out of the bathroom, pushing the children out into the hallway. I slammed the door shut.

'Good riddance tae him,' Jamesy shouted at the closed door. 'You could have had us all killed.'

'Jamesy,' I said, sighing, 'and Donald. Go to your bed.'

'Mother,' Donald ran and hugged me. 'You shouldn't put up with him.'

'And what else could I do?' I asked him.

'We could sleep in a tent in Arthur's Seat,' Jamesy said. 'The tinkers do, and they sell stuff round the doors.'

If it wasn't so sad and pitiful I might have laughed. 'We can just pray your own father grows better,' I said. 'We've a fine house here. We'd have no bath in a tent! Or table. Or cooker. Now go to bed. Go on.'

It wouldn't be the first night Willie Lockhart slept in the bathroom. I heard him groaning and coughing when I went to put dross over the coal fire. I stood by the fire and listened till Willie's groans turned to snores. Still I stood there, feeling the fire's warmth at my legs. Outside on the street I heard someone shout. I hoped Jane was safe and warm in her friend's house. I could still smell the faintest trace of gas. I opened another window.

I heard Mina calling from the bedroom. 'Is our faither dead?'

'Go to sleep, lassie,' I said. 'Nobody's dead.'

I picked my sewing bag from the floor where I had dropped it and put it carefully away. Then I took off my coat and put on my pinny. I knelt on the linoleum floor with a bucket of bleached water by my side and a floor cloth in my hands. I plunged the cloth into the water. Like a woman in a trance I scrubbed the floor. And while my hands guided the floor cloth my mind flew to a better place, a better time; when every day was blue sky and sunshine. Every plate was full. Every fire was burning. Every sleep was peaceful.

Or that is how the past had come to seem. And I needed it to be like that.

And there was Grace and Sadie and me taking our first Victoria holiday… the twenty fourth of May… the Queen's birthday…

It was to be a holiday for all and us servant girls could think and talk of nothing else for weeks leading up to it.

'What will we do – fancy? A whole day!'

'And what hat will we wear?'

'And could we take a boat out on the river d'ye think? Could we? Could we?'

'Aye,' we all chorus, 'oh aye!'

The twenty-fourth o' May,
it's the queen's birthday,

if we dinnae get a holiday
we'll a' run away!

I wake at five in the morning with these words skipping away in my head… *the queen's birthday!* I feel like a queen myself with a whole day's holiday. I lie in bed, watching the sky turn from dim grey to pale green then glowing peach. Lizzie the parlour maid, is still asleep. She told me, for her holiday, she planned to give herself a blessed long lie and stay in bed till nine o'clock then sit with her feet up all morning and write a letter to her mother. I lie there listening to her breathing. The '*twenty-fourth o' May, the queen's birthday*' chanting so loud inside me I think it's going to waken her.

If we dinnae get a holiday we'll a' run away! I can't lie abed any longer. I toss off the heavy grey blanket and wash at the wash stand. I love the sloshing sound the water makes spilling from the white jug. My heart is fluttering as I comb my hair and dress. I roll on my lisle stockings, button my dark green skirt and put on my clean linen blouse.

'You're right pretty, Johanna,' comes a voice. I almost jump out my skin. It's Lizzie, with one eye open and the other shut.

'Oh aye,' I say, shaking my head, but the truth is I feel pretty – with the sun sliding into the room, bouncing off the water in the bowl and me with my best clothes on.

Grace and I set out at half past seven and many's the happy servant we meet on the road. We wave to each other, wishing each other a happy Victoria Day. Sometimes as we dander along Grace and me talk about our work and the fiery temperament of the cook. Sometimes we walk in silence, just enjoying the hawthorn bushes in bloom, the bursting red poppies in the fields and the pink dog roses winking in the hedgerows. Sometimes, in time to our stepping, we sing;

Step we gaily on we go, heel for heel and toe for toe,
Arm in arm and row on row, all for Marie's wedding.

A grand walking song is Marie's wedding. Many the long mile is made easier with that song, and doubtless thoughts of our own wedding and whether we, like Marie, will have plenty bonnie bairns as weel.

By nine o'clock that May morning Sadie, Grace and me are strolling by the banks of the river Comrie. We're all wearing our wide brimmed bonnets and our Sunday bests, our long skirts and petticoats rustling as we walk. It's hard to say which amongst us is the cheeriest. Sadie has stories galore and news from home. Her little brother has joined the church choir because he sings like an angel. Grace tells us about a new pattern she has for a calf length skirt and Sadie says it's high time our bonny ankles got an airing. Sadie has more gossip from Cuthie Bank.

'He had a hand up her skirt – I saw it with my own eyes!'

'Did you run away?'

'I did! What d'ye take me for? I turned on ma heels, hoisted up my pinny and belted down that dark corridor. It's haunted I swear it is. They skimp on gas and candles and us servant girls aye have tae grope about in the dark. But you'll never find a stable boy up my skirt. I'll leather him first.'

'He'll go straight to hell,' I say, my hands to my cheeks, 'and roast.'

'That he will,' says Sadie, her voice a whisper as though any passers-by might string her up for gossip. 'And I'll tell you friends, it won't just be servant lads roasting and screaming – oh no – a guid few maisters will be down there too!'

'Not in Grange House,' says Grace, shaking her head. She can see I'm upset. Victoria Day holiday is spoiled already. 'No – ours is a good Christian house and the Balfours are respectable.' There is mother's word. I hold on to it, as though it can right a tipping ship. Respectable.

Still, it takes a good dander along the river bank, followed by a strong sweet cup of tea and a girdle scone with raspberry jam from the fete at the church hall to rid myself of the image of a red haired stable boy with his hand up the skirt of that poor milk-maid.

By noon we agree on hiring a rowing boat. The sky is blue and under it the glinting river laps slowly. Cherry blossoms drift over the water. She's like a bride the river is – all dressed up for Queen Victoria. Except the queen is dead.

Sadie knocks my hat off then runs away laughing. I dash after her, feeling like a child again. *If we dinnae get a holiday we'll a' run away!*

'We'll have to find a decent looking chap to row for us,' says Grace. We all lower our eyes as we approach the boat hiring shed. There are several men, all in white jackets and cream coloured trousers, seated on a bench outside the shed. These men are the rowers. It's Sadie who eventually points to the broad shouldered man with the fine head of black hair on him. 'Definitely the maist dependable chap I'd say,' she whispers and giggles behind her hand. We all glance at him then nod.

'We're trusting him wi' oor lives,' says Grace and we all whisper a quick petition to Saint Christopher.

Standing nervously on the stone step we hoist our long skirts to our knees. 'Steady now,' the rower calls out, his voice a deep bell of re-assurance. 'One by one ladies, there's no rush, give me your hand now, one by one.' He stands with one foot in the gently rocking boat and the other on the stone step, lifting his broad hand to each of us in turn. He is tall, with a sparkle in his blue eyes. 'There's room for all, ladies, and a happy Victoria Day to you.' We murmur shyly in reply, greeting him likewise, and Sadie, settling herself in the boat, giggles behind her hand. I feel how warm and strong his grip is. How slim and light my own hand in comparison. There will be no sinking in those dependable hands. 'I'd say you brought the sunshine with you,' he says straight to me, his voice deep and warm.

'Oh aye, we did that,' says Sadie, recovering from her fit of the giggles. 'We did that!' But it was me the man looked at, and I swear I've never seen such good and kind eyes nor have I ever felt the way his eyes made me feel. I want to keep looking at him, to never take my eyes away, but of course I flush pink in the face and lower my head, then it's me, giggling into my cupped hand.

We are not the only ones out on the river that day. 'This river is as busy as a carriage-way,' Sadie shouts out, and sometimes we wave to people passing.

'The Earn is a bonny river,' the handsome man says.

'Oh, it is,' I say, nodding and smiling. I am so happy. Again and again my gaze falls to the man's strong hands, his fingers firmly gripping around the oars and I see the ripple of his shoulder muscles under his jacket, with each pull of the oars. We could hit an iceberg and this boat wouldn't sink. We could run into pirates and he would keep us safe. Sometimes our eyes meet. He smiles at me and I smile back, wishing Sadie and Grace were gone, though feeling guilty for wishing so.

'I'm here every Sunday in the summer,' he says as he helps me out of the boat when the blissful ride is over. It's me he's speaking to. He looks clear at me and for all my shyness I look straight back. My heart skips a beat. I nod my head. I'm already thinking how the week after, in the four free hours we get after church, I'll run to him. I'll take a boat on my own. It will be just him and me on the river. I smile. And he holds my hand and gently squeezes it. 'Melville,' he says, 'Mr James Melville.'

'Blackie,' I whisper, 'Miss Johanna Blackie.'

***

When I got up from the floor my bones were stiff and the water was cold. I shivered what with all the chilled night time air coming in through the open windows. I wrung out my dirty floor cloth. I didn't have the strength to lug the bucket of filthy water down to the back green. I left it for the morning and went over to the window. The stars were out and there was a sliver of a moon. I stayed staring at it for a moment and felt tears prick my eyes. 'Now wheesht ye old fool,' I said to myself, 'wheesht.' Then I lowered that window, left the other one open, put out the light and went to bed.

It must have been past midnight by now but Gordon was still awake. 'Is he dead?' he whispered from his bed which was at the foot of our own.

'Wheesht laddie,' I said, lowering my head onto the pillow, 'nobody's dead. It was just an accident. Now go to sleep.'

25

Willie had a lump on his neck the size of a fist. Of course I noticed it. I'd often mentioned it and how I was sure it was growing but he wouldn't hear of doctors or hospitals. 'It's the fiddle,' he said, and for a while that seemed reason enough to ignore it. And little difference it would have made what I suggested, but I felt for him. Saw him grimace in pain and the way he frowned when swallowing his food. Drink now, that was a different thing entirely. 'That's why I drink, woman,' he said, pointing to the great boil on his neck.

Willie's wee shop was near the university and it seemed he had befriended a few medical students. If you believed him his watch-maker's shop was a hot-house of communist debate and poetry and the real university was in his shop. He came home one evening, the whiff of whisky strong on him. Only Gordon was at home that night. His brothers and sisters were spending Friday night with Auntie Jemima down at Granton. They helped her clean her house on Fridays. Doubtless Willie had remembered that.

Nothing was said until Willie had sprinkled his usual spoonful of curry powder onto his soup and taken a few spoonfuls of the broth I had made. After dabbing his chin with his napkin and clearing his throat, loudly, he said, 'send Gordon off to his bed,' though it was six o'clock and still daylight. Poor laddie hadn't even got half way through his soup. But he went, scowling at his father but not daring to disobey him. As soon as the door was shut and we were alone at the table Willie laid down his spoon, cleared his throat noisily again then said, 'I'll be needing this table. And you better bring towels. And keep the laddie quiet.'

'Heavens man. What are you on about? What d'ye mean, ye'll be needing the table and towels? What are you talking about?'

He lifted his spoon to his neck and pointed to the bulging lump. 'It's comin' oot!' he said, then carried on eating his soup.

'Ye canna be serious faither,' I spluttered but knew there would be no stopping Willie Lockhart. Some plan was afoot. I felt a knot in my stomach.

'Ye ken I wouldnae trust a hospital as far as I could throw it. But dinna fash yersel woman, it's proper trained medical students I've hired. And ye better get this place ready.' He looked at his pocket watch, 'because they'll be here soon.'

The bedroom door opened and there was Gordon, standing staring at us. 'I'm still hungry,' he said. Poor laddie. I hurried him back into his room, told him on no account was he to step out of that room then brought him some broken biscuits and a cup of milk.

While Willie set about anesthetising himself with what was left of his bottle of whisky I turned the kitchen into an operating theatre. I moved about in a daze, bringing out clean towels and setting them out on a chair. I filled two buckets of clean water and lined them up under the table, all the while telling myself I worried too much. They were medical students, weren't they? By this time Willie was half sozzled and singing a lament to his lump.

I shook out a white tablecloth and draped it over the table, moving about like a woman in a dream, or a nightmare. When the knock at the door came I opened it, gasping when I saw how young they were, eighteen or nineteen maybe, just boys. And nervous looking, I could tell. If they were trained medical students I was Rabbie Burns. They looked like they hadn't been in training for more than a month. They tried to put on a look of bravado, lifting themselves tall and squaring out their shoulders, but frightened eyes don't lie. 'Mrs Lockhart, we're here to see Mr Lockhart. He, he, made an appointment.' I was ready to slam the door on their juvenile faces but Willie was at my back and pulling them past me and into the house. He was swaying and slurring now, boldly assuring them he wouldn't feel a thing. 'Get the damn bloody shing oot,' he said, kicking off his boots, clambering up onto the table, tearing off his collar and dropping his braces, 'oot wi it!' He unbuttoned his shirt with a rip. Buttons popped. I didn't know what to do. I stood in the room with my hands over my face. The boys had to help him up. But eventually there he was, laid out on my kitchen table with his trousers on and his white string semmit vest. 'Oot,' he slurred, stinking of whisky, 'yank the damn shing oot!'

The boys glanced at each other. One of them held Willie's head while the other dabbed the lump with some foul smelling ointment. That done he produced a silver blade and raised it into the air. I stood in the corner, my hands clamped over my mouth. Willie was far gone now. The boy holding Willie's head whispered to the other one, 'just do it. Quick. A clean incision.'

And that's what he did.

Blood spurted up in the air like a fountain. Willie whimpered. 'Right, right, quick, the scalpel now,' said the one still holding Willie's head, his voice shaking. 'Scrape it out, all of it. Quick.' And the one with the knife, who had blood down his own shirt and blood running down his arm, took up a scalpel and set about gouging out the offending lump. I heard the awful sound of scraping flesh.

'You've killed him,' I screeched, but I didn't dare stop what they had started. I just stood in the corner of the kitchen staring and screaming, shouting over and over, 'you've killed him, you've killed him!' The lump was like a fat kidney. The boy scooped it out in bits and the rubbery bloody flesh landed in the hand towel I had laid out on the table. I could see the boys were panicking. They started arguing, their voices breaking with panic.

'That's not how you do it.'

'You must have punctured an artery.'

'The blood's not stopping.'

And I could only repeat, my voice hysterical, 'the blood's not stopping. You've killed him!' I stuffed my fist in my mouth to stop myself screaming.

They looked at me and never have I seen a look of such despair, such panic. They were way out of their depth and they knew it. The tumour, for that's what they were calling it, was lying in bits on the towel. 'We have to sew him up,' they said, 'that's what we have to do now.' But whatever they did the blood kept spurting and drunken Willie, his neck split open and pouring blood, was unaware of it all. The boys frantically dabbed towels to soak up the blood. Instantly the towels turned bright red.

'You've killed him,' was all I could say. The patient on the table didn't move.

'Do you have a telephone by any chance?' one of them asked. I shook my head. 'Well, is there a telephone box nearby?' I nodded and pointed up the street. While one of the boys stayed, holding Willie's open neck together with towels and his trembling hands, the other ran up the street to the phone box.

I wrung the towels out under the tap and watched the blood spill into the sink. I tore up sheets and made rags. We wrapped his bloody neck up like a mummy but still the blood gushed everywhere.

I heard a car outside. The front door flew open. The student ran in and behind him stormed a black man. I couldn't believe it. In he came with his dark face, dark eyes, red mouth. And this black doctor was fuming. He looked at the bloody sight on the kitchen table and bellowed at the boys. He tore off his jacket and let it fall on the floor. Oh how the curtains up and down the street would be twitching. For the man in our house had a motor car, and, jings, crivens, he was black! From Africa!

The students were shame-faced and couldn't do enough to help. Now it was they wringing out towels and bringing pails of clean water, saying yes sir, no sir. The doctor worked quickly. He sewed up Willie's neck and stemmed the bleeding. 'You bloody idiots,' the doctor said in his strong deep voice. He tightened his stitching and the needle flashed in his quick hands.

'Aye, oh, sorry, sorry sir.'

'I have never –ever – seen such a terrible mess. Like a slaughter-house. That's what it is!'

'Sorry sir, it was just, the blood sir, kept gushing.'

'And where is the tumour then?'

The boys looked around. Where was it? I pointed under the table, my hand over my mouth to stop the sickness that heaved in my stomach. They all looked down. Bits of red rubbery flesh, hacked at, lay scattered under the table. 'Um, must have fallen in the panic of it all, sir,' said one of the boys.

'Have they killed him?' I wailed, sick with the stink and the sights.

The doctor pressed his hand over Willie's heart then looked slowly up at me. 'No,' he said, 'they haven't.'

And suddenly it was all over. The doctor and the students washed their hands in the kitchen sink then left. I heard the car engine roar up the road. I looked around at this kitchen of mine. It was a battlefield. Blood was everywhere. Willie lay unconscious on the table, but well stitched and breathing. The fire was still burning in the grate. I took up the bloody towels and the sheets and fed them into the fire, my hands shaking. The flames roared and leapt up. Everything was red. I fed the tumour into the fire. Then I set about scrubbing every trace of this horror away. When I thought Gordon was asleep I lifted Willie through to bed and got him into his nightshirt. Then I burned his vest and his trousers in the fire.

'What happened?' Gordon asked, his voice a whimper coming from under the blankets.

'Nothing happened,' I said. 'Now go to sleep.'

Then I went through to the bathroom, filled the bath though all hot water had been used up. I lay in the cold water and washed Willie's blood off me.

Before I finally got to bed that night I inspected the kitchen. Apart from a tiny dark stain on the floor all traces of blood were gone. No-one would ever know what had taken place this night. Even the lump on Willie's neck was gone.

26

The day I turn thirteen I'm sitting in front of the fire with a school book about the different kinds of fish you might catch in Scottish rivers.

I don't think it is interesting – but just to hold a leather bound book and sit in front of the fire turning the pages – now that is a fine thing. It must be a Sunday. People who come in stare at me, whistle – even though there's some folks frown upon anyone whistling on a Sunday – and say no doubt I'll be the first Blackie in history to go to the university.

'My damn arse,' says faither, not caring a whit about cursing or whistling on the Holy day, 'and wit's she still doin at that school anyway?'

'It's the law,' mother says, 'till they're fourteen,' half in pride and half in irritation, as though it was fine having a lassie doing well at the school, but it would be even better having her bringing in a bob or two.

'Christ almighty Jane. Fourteen? There wis me pit oot at ten and ma ain faither who niver even went tae the school at a'. So wit's she gonna dae wi a' that book stuff? She's a lassie fir Christ's sake. Gonnae breed and keep the hoose. Wit does she need books fir?'

'Teacher says she's neat Tam, an she could be a teacher. Says oor Johanna's got promise.'

'Och aye. Just gie's a lassie fancy thoughts o' herself and maks her ken wit she's no gonna get. The Blackie's are no toffs tae go eating porridge off a siller spoon and never will be Jane. The sooner she's oot that school the better.'

I know he's right. It's my birthday. I sit there with my book heavy in my hands and it seems suddenly like so much rot. Fishing in the highlands? What does fishing in the highlands mean to me? And what are the highlands anyway? And what is a book for? I have watched my mother and father and brothers and sisters and aunts and uncles and neighbours work their fingers to the bone. That's real. That makes a difference to folk. You can see it. The house is clean with mother's constant scrubbing. I have food in my belly with her constant cooking. I have clean clothes on my back and well I know the hours and effort it takes to make them clean.

'Well, Johanna's a rare wee worker anyway,' mother says, crossing her arms over her floury pinny. I look up from my book to where she stands in the kitchen, making scones for the Sunday visitors, and it strikes me how old she looks. Her hair is grey, pinned back any old how and bundled into a net with straggly bits poking out. Her hips are narrow and her breasts droop.

I notice how her mouth goes down at the sides and how her skin is wrinkly with broken red veins across her cheeks. Work, I think, makes her like that, down on her knees, scrubbing, and up and down these stairs carrying things, and over that tub cleaning, and at that range cooking. Work for my sake. And suddenly I feel a lump rise in my throat that hurts, thinking how my own mother wears herself down to the bone so I can look smart and clean and I love her for it. Love, I learn then, is an ache in your heart.

I snap the book shut and put it on the floor, pushing it away from me as if I might catch a germ off it.

'Do you want me to clean the windows?' I ask, jumping up, 'they're right dusty.'

'On a Sunday?' Mother looks at her visitors who shrug. It's all the same to them. 'Aye well, go on, be quick about it. You're a good help tae me Johanna. Wee princess.'

27

It was a windy day in early spring. I had cleaned the windows with newspaper and vinegar and the morning sunlight flooded the kitchen. I gazed out to the bulky hill of Arthur's Seat, thinking how bonny it all was. How Craigmillar looked fine that morning, all new. How my own kitchen looked fine too. The sun threw shadows onto the cracked deep sink and lit up dust motes in the air. I gazed at that sink, thinking, half in a dream, that the threads of cracked stone looked like rivers drawn in some old map. The Forth, the Tay, the Clyde and the Earn. I had a duster in my hand, ready to buff up the windows, but was taking a breather. My arm was sore. Even for a young woman, which I wasn't, cleaning windows was hard work. That's when I heard the postman's footsteps on the stairs. I heard the push and squeak of the letter box, a flapping followed by the quiet thud of a letter dropping onto the bare wooden floorboards in the lobby. My heart sank. I clutched the duster. Debts. That's what raced through my mind. More debts. I'd already emptied the tin I kept for emergencies.

Suddenly my mood lifted. I loosened my grasp of the duster. Maybe it's a letter from James Melville? My heart skipped a beat. It could be! Grace who came to visit just the day before told me *by the by,* he may not have died. The way she said it you'd think it was the weather she was talking about. 'Oh, you'll never guess, Johanna,' was how she brought up the subject when the two of us were taking our cup of tea. 'Word is going the rounds that your handsome boatsman from Comrie may have survived the terrible war after all.' I held my tea cup tight. My heart pounded in my ribs. What was she saying? 'Aye, he'd been in hospital a long time, so this woman who came into the club yesterday said. She couldn't be sure, but she thought so. Aye, but the man is much changed, she said, and gone so he would talk to no-one. She said he was like a bearded hermit living in his mother's house. Oh, and he's got one leg shorter than the other.' Grace paused to sip her tea. 'She was probably mistaken,' she added, smiling at me. 'And I wouldn't heed her Johanna, she's a terrible gossip. It was probably somebody else.'

With trembling fingers I put my cup down, scared I would let it crash to the floor. Under the table I twisted my hands. My stomach churned. I gripped the underside of the table, scared I might fall to the floor. 'It might be him, then,' I said, my voice coming out small and anxious. 'It could be.'

'It could, aye, and what of it?' She reached for another biscuit.

'I… I could go to him.' In that moment I knew I would cross the ocean in a ship for him. I felt a leap in my heart, like a candle. 'To see, if it is him.'

'You always were a dreamer, eh, Johanna?'

How could she say that? I had five children. And was down on my knees cleaning and scrubbing every day. I was forever working. And as if that wasn't harsh enough I had Willie Lockhart to cope with. And she called me a dreamer? I shook my head and lowered my voice to a whisper, 'no Grace. I believe in love. If that makes me a dreamer, well, then I am. You closed your heart, Grace, and I can't say I don't understand you.'

Now it was Grace looked down and shook her head. 'We're both of us getting on, Johanna. We're both trying to make the best of things.'

I wanted her to say more about James Melville, but didn't trust my voice. Grace finished her tea, dabbed her lips with the napkin then thanked me for the tea. 'Even if it was true,' she said, folding her napkin, 'which, more than likely it's not, what difference would it make, after all these years?'

All the difference in the world, I wanted to say. Instead I looked down into the dregs of my tea cup, to see if James Melville was still alive. The leaves clumped into the letter J. I felt hope leap inside me.

Then, telling me she had a bus to catch Grace up and left. After she was gone I let the tea things sit on the table. A rare flame burned in me again. I suddenly remembered a pink dog-rose floating down the wishing river. I let myself sit for a bit then slowly rose and washed the cups, telling myself to see sense.

But what if this woman was right? An image of a wounded soldier came to me. Much changed. Bearded hermit. Home from the war. I would care for him. I would love him.

With the childish hope that the letter might be from him I ran through to the hallway. For a moment I stared at it, a white oblong shape on the dark floor. Trembling I bent down to pick the letter up. It was a good white envelope. I turned it over and stared at the stamp. United States of America, it said, with the blue and red of the stars and stripes. Surely James Melville did not emigrate to America?

I weighed the letter in my hand. Who did I know in America? I had many half-brothers and sisters but couldn't think of any who had gone out to America. By the typed print on the envelope I could see this letter was official. I could also see it was addressed to my husband. Did Willie have a debt in America? Who knows where he'd been before I met him?

I took a deep breath and carried the letter through to the kitchen. Though it was light it weighed heavily in my hand. I had managed to deal with Willie's debts before. Doubtless I'd manage again. A shiver of guilt ran through me for opening a letter addressed to someone else, but I'd seen too many such letters, all of them addressed to Mr Lockhart. Rent arrears. Unpaid bills. Seeing to debts was just another of our unspoken arrangements. With shaking fingers I took up a knife. With one fast cut I slit the envelope.

The letter quivered in my hand. Standing by the sink I read;

Dear Mr William Lockhart

Sadly we inform you of the death of your wife.

Mrs Rubena Lockhart, from Haddington, East Lothian, Scotland, died peacefully at home on the 5th March 1935 in Pennsylvania, United States of America. Your daughter, Faith Lockhart, is executor of your late wife's estate.

We regret to be the informants of this sad news

Macdonald Rooke

Underwriters

The letter fluttered in my hand like a live trapped bird. This couldn't be right. My throat closed up. There must be some mistake. I coughed. I felt I would choke. I read the letter again, then again. I felt a grip like a huge fist around my chest. I struggled to breathe. Auntie Faith! The comics from America. The gossips in Haddington. His age and all the other lies. I dropped the letter, felt that clawing hand sink to grip my stomach. I grasped the cold edge of the sink, leant into it and vomited over the map of rivers. Again and again I retched. Then I fell to my knees and wept.

By the time Willie announced his presence, bawling out his favourite song on the street, I had wiped my tears, blown my nose and said my prayers. I sat silently at the table, staring at the letter which lay open, its edges already curling in. I felt hollow inside. Who was I if I wasn't Mrs Lockhart? For once my hands sat slumped on the table, idle. From down on the street his song slammed into me.

'*So comrades come rally!*' Willie was near the house. '*And the last fight let us face.*' I heard him open the door and plod up the stone steps. I pictured his fist punching the air. The song carried on, muffled in the stairwell, breathless; '*the Internationale... unites...*' I heard him barge into the house. He was still singing in the lobby. Well I knew the words. '*The human race....*' The song died on his lips. I heard him splutter. Heard his hands curl around the letter. Crush the paper in his hand. Then I heard the letter crackle in the fire.

Now I stared at emptiness. For the first time in sixteen years there was no soup bubbling on the fire. There was no potted herrings or semolina on the range. There was nothing. The table was not set. Bastards; that's the word that clawed at me, jeered and shrieked in me. Bastards! And if they were bastards, these five good bairns, what did that make me? A nothing. A whore. A slut. A woman in sin. A mistress.

I could smell the singed hot stink of strong tobacco. So Willie was in his chair by the fire, pulling on his pipe. If he wept for his wife he did it in the pub that night. The children, doubtless aware of the terrible mood, stayed away. I heard them playing on the street. I heard their feet scuffling on the road. I heard Gordon bawl for a moment. He must have tripped. Normally I'd be up at the window like a shot, and I'd lift it, and call out to the bairns on the street below – 'watch what you're doing will you! Are you alright son? Come up and get a bandage on that graze.' Not today. Bastard, that's what they'll call you son, bastard.

Willie, seeing there was to be no supper this night, rose to leave. I looked up then, hearing him take his bowler hat down from the sideboard where it lay. 'Well?' was all I could say, my throat dry as tinder and my voice cracking. I said it again, and again. Once I started I couldn't stop. 'Well? Well? Well?' It was the only word I could utter though nothing was well and would ever be well again. I felt shamed to my bones. My very blood was tainted. 'Well?'

'I thocht she wis deed.' He shut the door and went out into the night.

My whole body felt frozen. I felt nothing anymore, just numb with cold. The coal scuttle needed filling. The dinner needed making. Still the bairns stayed away. Were they even my bairns? Was there any legal bond between us? That stirred me into feeling. I glanced up, afraid. What if they took my children away? I am Miss Blackie am I not? I am not Mrs Lockhart. Mrs Lockhart is dead. Rubena Lockhart died peacefully at home. The name drummed in my head. Rubena – from Haddington! God in heaven, ten years I suffered in that place. Ten years and all that time everyone must have known. The way Clara coughed in the church the day we were married. All those years – she knew.

Still I sat there. The fire had gone out. It was dark outside now. Silently the children came in, hardly children anymore most of them. Jane was nearly fifteen. They stood in the doorway and looked at me. I couldn't meet their gaze. I couldn't bring myself to tell them this most awful shameful thing. I wanted to die, right there. I wanted the floor boards to crack open and take me. But I didn't hold with lying. I didn't hold with dishonesty. So I told them.

I lowered my eyes and stared the whole time down at my hands. I twisted my cheap cheating wedding ring round and round on my finger. Tears now splashed onto my hands. Not one for telling lies, did I say? I was kidding myself. 'It was a very long time ago,' I heard myself saying, my voice as though from a long way off, 'and faither thought she was dead. He married me thinking she was dead. And – auntie Faith. Well now, isn't life a mystery at times. She's your sister.'

I couldn't say more. It was out. The words had been spoken and as softly as I knew how. By their silence and gasps I knew they were stunned. Still I couldn't bring myself to look at them. Bastards; that would be the word crying in their poor hearts.

'Ye'll be hungry mother,' was what Donald said, breaking the silence. 'Let's have some bread and margarine.'

'And jam on it,' chirped Gordon. The whole sorry tale was beyond his years.

'Aye, and I'll fetch up some coal from the bunker,' said Jamesy. 'It's cold mother.' And that word sustained me. Whatever I was not I was surely still their mother.

We'd get through this like we'd got through everything else. Donald put a hand on my shoulder and said the word again – 'mother.' I let myself cry good and proper then. Buckets of tears. The table cloth was soaked with them. And I cried not only for this shame but for so many. The shames I'd borne and told no-one about. Who could I tell how it is to be married to an old drinking man – or not married and for nigh on sixteen years believing you are married? And for my own father that day when he lay in the street shouting my name. Threepence; that was all I gave him. And I cried for my own mother. I knew what she endured because I endured it too. I must have cried for a full half hour without stopping – my heart breaking into a thousand pieces. Then I heard the old brown kettle whistling on the gas ring.

'Rhubarb jam mother,' said Jane, setting a door-stop of a slice of bread down in front of me and a steaming hot cup of tea. 'That's your favourite isn't it – rhubarb?'

It wasn't but I nodded. Raspberry was my favourite but this was no time to be saying so. Despite everything, I wiped my tears, looked up at my eldest daughter, and smiled. 'Aye, rhubarb,' I said, 'so it is.'

28

I row down that blue river a thousand times.

I feel his strong arms wrapped around me. I can see them, broad and capable, when I close my eyes, setting a fire, wiping down a table, stitching an apron, skinning a rabbit. His eyes are as real as the sky. I feel warm with the feeling that, with arms such as these to help me, I will never be cold, never have to carry more than I can manage. There will always be someone dependable to share the load. Always be someone to catch me if I fall.

'Our boys are coming home, Blackie,' says Baxter and I cheer with the rest of them. But they're not coming home to us. And the one boy I care about isn't coming home. If the news is true, and I hope to God in heaven it's not true. I want to tear out the cruel tongues that say most of the 51st Highland battalion was wiped out.

'Be proud you have done your duty, Blackie,' Mrs Wakeford tells me. 'No-one serves their country better than a servant.'

'Aye,' says Baxter, tears in her eyes, 'we've kept Britain alive! We kept the home fires burning!' Then she nudges me and taps her finger to her nose. Lowering her voice to a whisper she says, 'you well might see your sweetheart again, for they're not all dead. Have hope Blackie.' Leaving me stunned she returns to waving a little Union Jack and cheering.

First chance I get to talk to her on her own I ask her what news she has heard. 'No news, exactly,' she says, winking at me, 'mair a woman's instinct,' and she pats her stomach as though that's where instinct lies, and for some reason I think of tea leaves, and palm readings.

The general elation and parties in the street for the end of the war fair gets to Mr Wakeford. The atmosphere of victory seems to give him new vigour. 'We've won,' he keeps shouting, punching a fist in the air, then he tries to grab me. I don't like to find myself in a room on my own with him. They're neither of them in their prime and the old man is having, what Grace calls, a second childhood. 'Well, I didn't go around slapping folk's bottoms in my childhood,' I say, crying because he's done it again.

Grace, for all her dignity, seems to accept things like that as part of the job. 'You make sure there's nothing about your uniform can give the wrong impression, no strain for the buttons, no tightness over the hips or any sort of frippery. Then you pass along the corridor quick as you can Johanna, or you give way on the stairs and stand well back, and you pay it no heed. In fact, you pretend it didn't happen.'

'Aye, that's the way of it,' Baxter chimes in. It's dinner time and war or no war I can't eat. I push my small plate of boiled hough away and Baxter is quick to take it from me. 'Waste not, want not. No wonder you're lovely and slim. No wonder he slaps your bottom. Look at you – and that photograph you showed me, a wee film star that's what you are. I tell you Blackie, I'd be fair delighted if Mr Wakeford slapped my bottom – delighted.'

'Well, it's not Christian – that kind o' thing,' I say and burst into tears all over again.

'Och, Christian. Damn it Blackie. Lassies are great temptations for men and it's no just men's fault. Look at us, wi' our paps and our shapely bottoms – well – you I mean, not me of course. Oh no, not me. Who would look at ugly old Baxter?'

Then Grace has to comfort her while I clear away the lunch plates with a good deal of banging and clattering. By rights Baxter is supposed to clear up the lunch things. Grace is needed to serve afternoon tea upstairs and I'll soon have my hands steeped in laundry for hours, plus I run messages, plus I lay the fires, plus I help Baxter out with cooking sometimes and washing up to say nothing of the toilet. But I am not fourteen anymore – I am twenty four. I've been in service ten years. I too have dignity. The boys are coming home to marry their sweethearts and I am left on the shelf. I swing round and raise my voice at Baxter;

'I might be a servant but I'm not your servant. And I might be a laundry maid and I might not have a husband o' my own but that doesn't gie any man the right to clap his sweaty hands over me.' I bang the plates down into the sink, tear off my apron, leave it lying in a heap on the scullery floor and run, blinded with tears, up the stairs and out the front door. The Wakefords are having their after lunch nap in their armchairs in the drawing room and there he is, the dirty old man, dribbling away, heedless of the pain he has caused.

I run along the leafy avenue then stop at the corner and blow my nose. I feel so stupid. Here I am, a grown woman acting like a spoilt child. Grace is right – a wee bit slap on the bottom is harmless enough, and Baxter is tired, anyone can see that. It is easy enough for me to help her out. What is all the fuss about?

Loneliness, that's what it is, but I just stuff that ache down inside me and bury it as deep as I can. Thankfully at that moment Grace appears and seeing me her usual properness and dignity melts. 'Johanna,' she says putting her hands in mine and squeezing them tight. 'Be strong dear Johanna.'

We walk back arm in arm. Baxter is singing God save the King while she's getting on with the lunch dishes. The Wakefords are still sound asleep.

That afternoon, rubbing woollen blankets in hot soapy water harder than I need to I can feel the breaking feeling again. I remember it from before – like when the games ended, when the street stopped singing, when the school learning came to an end. Now another thread is coming loose and as I work, my back bent over the tin bucket full of steamy blankets, I feel I am dissolving. I love my work. I have loved it for ten years. It brings me order and satisfaction. It makes my world clean and gives it meaning. By the time all the blankets are washed and rung through the mangle I know this way of life is coming to an end. Call it the second sight or Baxter's woman's knowing, but that day I know my life is about to change drastically. And with a knot in the pit of my stomach I know the road ahead has nothing to do with James Melville. What now, I wonder. What now?

When I have time off I sometimes go home to Gordon Street. To see my own mother, with bright red lipstick painted over her thin lips, you'd think she is almost enjoying the war. I think it's the cinema. It gives her a new lease of life. Even her hair looks nice and curled as though she's bothered. They've got the electricity into Gordon Street and after all, mother says, it's cleaner and as long as you keep the meter fed you're fine and how bright the house looks with not a cobweb in sight. 'So ye've come back tae see yer auld mither,' she says and I smile. It's Sunday afternoon and a good while since I've managed back.

'We're getting a carpet sweeper,' mother says, as proud as I've ever seen her, her arms folded and her scarlet lips puckered. 'So what d'ye think aboot that then?'

'That's rare,' I say, 'you'll be getting the appliances and even a motor car next.'

'Hardly!' But the way she chirps the word I am wondering if maybe she doesn't already have a fine black motor car parked on Gordon Street.

'Never you mind motor car,' mother says, then tells me I'll miss the bus if I don't hurry up. 'The marrying bus,' she says, laughing loudly at her joke. 'Ken how many British soldiers have gone off tae this war JoHann?' mother's cronies tell me. 'Three and a half million! Ha! If that's no making a country o' spinsters nothing will.' Mother, me and her cronies are huddled round the tea pot. 'Ach, go on Johann,' mother's nudging my elbow. 'Let Jessie here have a keek at yer tea leaves. See if yer gone tae be a spinster for the rest o yer life. Or mibbe that old gardener mannie that prunes the roses ye telt us aboot; him that's aye ogling ye, mibbe he's fir ye.'

So I upturn my tea cup and who comes sailing into my heart and mind but James Melville. Jessie peers over the pattern of brown leaves and whistles. All the time I am hoping it isn't Mrs Wakeford's old gardener she is seeing in the pattern of brown leaves. But I don't pull my hand away like I should. Jessie's good at tea-leaves. There are folks in Gordon Street even pay Jessie, in kind, to do their tea-leaves. And I am twenty four. Almost twenty five. There are women my age and younger already resigned spinsters. Is there a man out there, home from the war and waiting for me? Rowing a boat towards me? I remember the feel of the scrape of coal across my forehead. I have been taught not to hope.

'Aye, like yer faither,' Jessie says, pushing my cup away, 'and no as handsome either. But a rake o' bonny bairns to make up for it.' She stares at me strangely for a second then quickly looks away.

I cough, pull my hand away from her grasp and plunge it into my lap, under the table. Tosh, I imagine Grace saying, pagan tosh. Mother and her cronies are forever reading tea-leaves. They've got superstitions for everything. God himself will strike you down if you put your shoes on the table. Wear red and green together and risk hell-fire. Jessie glances at me, takes a swig of cold tea then quickly changes the subject.

Their favourite subject, after Mrs Wakeford, is Charlie Chaplin! While they chat about the latest film they have seen I clutch at the waist band of my skirt, pulling at it as though I am struggling to breathe. There is no way on God's earth I will marry a man like my faither. Tosh. Pagan tosh!

'I have to go,' I say, getting to my feet. 'I have to get back.'

'But we haven't telt ye about The Empire yet JoHann. Jings lassie, the pictures is just great. I went wi' Elsie to see the new Charlie Chaplin. It's called The Tramp. Oh, what a mannie he is. What a mover! Course, you'll no have the freedom tae go to the pictures working all the hours o' the day and night for yer baldy lady.' Mother and Jessie laugh while I pull my coat on, trying to laugh with them but not managing.

'Cheerio then,' I say, opening the door. The cold air from the landing hits at my face.

'Aye – dinnae keep baldy toff waiting. Aff and brush that wig. Cheerio!'

I walk back through the streets of Leith, my head spinning. Every step I take feels like a step towards the man Jessie saw in my cup. A man, like father, who is standing on some street corner, with a rake of bairns, waiting for me. I glance into the face of the few men I pass, wondering if that's him; the one I am fated to marry. If they glance back at me I quickly look down, or hurry on. One man even winks at me and doffs his cap. Then to my horror he starts to follow me.

I lift up my skirts and run. I hear his footsteps quicken behind me. I want to cry. I run faster but Sunday clothes are an ill fit for running in. The streets are deserted. Being Sunday all the shops are closed. Usually the fishwives from Newhaven are out on the streets, crying their wares, but not on a Sunday. Or if the weather's fair families might be out walking, but this day is grey. It has started to spit rain and precious few folks are out walking. Then I hear his voice call to me. By now he's right behind.

'Was it me you was looking for?' He sounds desperate – but just lonely, not violent. 'Wis it? Wis it me?'

I turn around, my heart thudding. I stare at him and shake my head. 'No,' I say, panting and stepping back, 'no – I – I thought maybe, you – were my brother.' Lies come easily. The man's face falls. I see him look over my shoulder, anxious, as though my brother might suddenly appear. 'He's due back from the war – my brother is. Leave me alone.' I turn and run again. Thankfully this time he doesn't follow. This time there are no steps behind me.

By the time I reach Trinity I am shaking like a leaf and it's Mrs Wakeford herself who comforts me with a plate of oxtail soup. 'Think yourself lucky,' she says, when I tell her a man followed me along Constitution Street. 'It's been a while since any fellow ran after me.' I dab at my tears then eat the soup. I made the soup the day before. It tastes good. With every spoonful I feel stronger, yet still I can't rid my thoughts of Jessie's predictions. Would my husband, I wonder, like the taste o' my soup?

***

Three days later I walked up the street to the telephone box and in a feeble voice that I struggled to lift above a whisper made an appointment with the registrar. Speak up, he kept saying, I can't hear you! 'Married,' I said, holding my other hand over the mouth piece as though I was a war time spy. 'I wish to be married.'

The banns would need to be displayed for fourteen days, I was told. Only then, if no-one came forward with any objections, could I be married. Where, I wondered, were the objections sixteen years ago? Speak now or forever hold your peace, isn't that what is said? I don't remember the minister saying those words sixteen years ago. He must have. That's when Clara took her coughing fit I supposed.

For two weeks I went about my duties and spoke hardly a word. I dreaded another wife would appear – from America, Australia, Glasgow? And these public banns were posted in the registrar's window in Newington. Some gossiping neighbour would be sure to see the announced forthcoming wedding of William Lockhart, widower, and Miss Johanna Blackie. The fear of being found out kept me awake at nights.

Willie kept away from the public house and took to playing melancholy airs on his violin. I could see how the children shut themselves up. Here was another secret they would carry around with them. Father took no well at times; that was our shared lie. That made drunkard easier to swallow. Our father's not a drunk, they said to friends in school, oh no, not a drunkard. It's just our poor faither doesn't keep too well. It was the war you ken, and the boil on his neck.

Now here was another one they'd have to deal with; bastard, bigamist. I watched them sew that shame up inside them. For the world outside they dressed the lie up to make it easier to live with, because too well I knew it, folk would find out. Oh aye, oor faither was married before – a long time back. Then the war came and he went to fight. She, poor woman, thinking he was killed, went away. He, coming back, thought she was dead. So he married again. Who wouldn't? He thought she was dead, see.

A good story. I managed not to drown by believing it more and more each day. I made Willie a war hero and Rubena, pregnant and beautiful, a distressed widow who took free passage to the New World. Of course there were huge holes in my story. Comics from America for instance. So why did Rubena leave Willie? Did she manage to do what I failed to do? I never asked him. If I was to ask I'd admit her existence. Then she would come in and live like a ghost in our house; the true wife; Rubena. I pursed my lips, and as much as was possible, carried on as before.

The bunting is going up across the streets and the Union Jacks are lifted high.

Women who went off to work in the factories are smoking cigarettes in long gold holders and the twenties are round the corner and ready to roar. The in word is 'improvement' and ankles are all the fashion. The men are coming home and they're not all dead like I thought they'd be – but you see a dull film over their eyes where youth used to be.

The whole of Scotland is singing, even though 70,000 Scottish soldiers lie dead in France. The Wakefords give Grace and myself two days holiday. And though Grace shakes her head and tells me nothing good will come of it I take a bus the long journey to Perthshire. I have to know. I have read again and again how the 51st highland division lost so many brave soldiers, first in 1914 on the Western Front, then in May 1915 at the battle of Ypres. And how so many of the dead are buried in the north of France. But I can't believe James is dead. I believe he has made it home, and suffers because he doesn't know where I am. I am wearing my best clothes. I am tongue tied and sick with nerves. And if I do find him, sad and crippled, what then? What will I ever find to say? But I have this horrible black feeling inside me. It follows me all the way on the long bus journey. People are singing on the bus but I can't join in. And when finally I arrive at the pretty and tranquil village of Comrie I run the two miles down to the river. The boats are still there, tethered to the bank. Four long years have passed. My hair spills out of my hat and I don't care. I am breathless, hot, with mud on my boots.

But I see him; the same old man. He is painting the boating shed. The paint is dark green. Hearing me he turns and holds the paint brush in the air. Green splats of paint fall back into his paint pot. He looks at me as if he remembers me. The black feeling wells up then. It is going to pull me under. I am going to drown. He steps back. I watch the old man lower his paint brush slowly into a jar of turps. He shakes his head at me then speaks. 'My son didn't make it. We waited. Letters he wrote, then they stopped. After the battle of the Somme the letters stopped. He didn't make it. Twenty one, that's what he was. A hero…' The man can't carry on. He wrings his hands together and his face breaks.

'And, James Melville?' I ask. 'Is there news?'

The man just stares at me, as if he doesn't understand what I am saying. 'He didn't make it,' he says again, with tears in his eyes, and I clutch at my skirt, spin round and run. I have heard enough. I don't even say I am sorry about his son. I race over the grass. Then outside the village I stop, my breath coming hard and fast. I need to keep him alive. In my heart and in my thoughts I will keep him alive. I will keep him strong and young.

But I have my life to live. And so I take the bus back to Edinburgh, vowing on that long bumpy journey I will move on. I will put my feet on the ground. I won't be a dreamer. That's what Grace is always calling me. But that night she holds me in her arms when I cry. That Sunday I sing every hymn for him. It soothes the ache inside me. After that I vow I won't think of him anymore. Though that vow lasts only an hour or so and then I am searching for my precious paper. I am dipping my pen in a bottle of ink.

17 Dovecot Brae
Trinity
Edinburgh
13th November 1918

My dear James

So, it ended, this bloody war. We won! They are stringing up bunting in Edinburgh and the streets are gay with a riot of red, white and blue. I miss you. Some soldiers are returning home. They wear brave faces but I see no light in their eyes. And their youth is gone. 70,000 Scottish soldiers are dead.

Am I writing this to a ghost then?

If the unthinkable is true, I would still love you. And pray we would then be together in the hereafter.

But I don't believe you are dead. Grace says I must put you from my mind. I will soon be twenty five and practically an old maid. She says I must find someone soon if I want to be married, and have children.

Tears blur my eyes and these words blot. There, I have smudged my sentence.

The last letter I sent was returned with the words – no longer at this address. So James, I wrapped it in tissue and placed it at the bottom of my kist. I will keep them for you. These letters will be a way to pull back the lost years. And anyway, it soothes my soul to write to you. To imagine you.

Everything is changing. Do you know, they have contraptions for sweeping the rugs and only yesterday, I admit I was dreaming, but a motor car very nearly sent me tumbling. It's all modern this and modern than. But in my heart's eye I see you rowing me down a peaceful river into blessed eternity. I hear the river lapping as I lay down weary to sleep. Of course, it isn't the river Comrie but the Firth of Forth. It is quite close to Trinity.

Come home soon
With love
Johanna

29

The following week the Wakeford's are entertaining for the end of the war. Folks they haven't seen for months are to come and dine. And I am sent to the butchers for chops.

There's a long queue in the butchers and it is like a concert going on in there. People are singing, cheering and slapping each other on the back. The shop is festooned with paper Union Jacks and you can't help feeling lifted by the jolly celebration mood. On the other side of the counter five burly men in blood streaked blue overalls chop and cleave and chat away. My coat hides my apron but doubtless everyone can tell by looking at me I am a servant. I am well practised in lowering my eyes and giving way. I am not the sort to be joining in all this singing and laughing in the butchers but I enjoy it fine all the same.

I can't help but notice a man in uniform– just ahead of me in the queue, who seems to be entertaining the whole shop. He has a fine strong voice and is belting out – *come fill up my cup and come fill up my can.* His singing plus the busy, cheery atmosphere reminds me of the wee parties years back in Gordon Street. For a moment I forget myself and join in, clapping the beat and tapping my foot on the wooden floor with the rest of them.

That's when the soldier turns round and beams at me. Staring into folk's eyes is something I was taught not to do, but this man's eyes are like fish hooks and even though my cheeks are flaming crimson I can't help myself. I hold his gaze as he continues to stare at me. He stops singing, even though everyone in the shop carries on. Brown his eyes are, like ploughed earth. The song whirrs around us while this soldier man stares at me and I stare back. His eyes are wide as tea-cups. Then he shakes his head in disbelief and his face opens into a wide smile.

'The lassie in the photie!' he exclaims, laughing. Flushed, I quickly lower my eyes to the floor but he keeps on laughing regardless. Father hates vanity. If he gets to know about the photo doubtless he'll tear it up. Now I feel exposed and want to die of shame. 'You're the lassie in the window up in the town,' he says. 'I'd ken you anywhere.' My cheeks are on fire and I swallow hard. I don't know what to say. The photographer must have liked my photograph. He must have developed one for himself and placed it in the shop window, using it to advertise his skills. All this races through my mind, a mixture of pride and shame. But the man now staring at me won't stop, won't leave me alone – next thing he turns and tells the whole butcher's shop about me. 'Ladies and gentlemen,' he shouts, 'would you believe it! I lost my heart tae a photograph and here she in – in the flesh. A servant, and here wis me thinking she wis a film star!'

Then everybody laughs and hoots and I want to turn on my heels and run. But something keeps me there. With my heart hammering wildly in my chest I fold my hands together and keep my head down. For once I don't run. I stand my ground and say nothing, breathing deeply to compose myself. When I feel brave enough to glance up first thing I notice is a row of gleaming medals the length of his lapel, and this soldier man, still gaping at me in what looks like admiration.

'I was thinking o' getting a photograph taken masel,' the man is saying, to me and to everyone, like he's on a stage. 'Aye, you never know when your number's up and it would be an awfy shame to go to heaven, or the other place, without a photograph.' Then he shuffles in closer to me and presses his mouth close up to my ear and whispers 'I'll take you to the Ross Bandstand on Saturday.' I flush red again. I shake my head. But I have to marry sometime. I can't be in the Wakeford's house for ever and not with all these machines coming. And he is a soldier. He has won the war.

'Or does a fine lassie like yersel no go fir the Scotch music? It's grand so it is. Come wi me lassie. Come wi a Scottish soldier.' Then what does he do then but burst into song again and start marching in a four by four beat all around the butcher's. And doesn't he come right round behind me and brush his knees up against my skirt. I edge forward but the place is that packed there's little space to move. He has a lovely voice.

'Will ye?' he says, cocking his head to one side and staring into my eyes.

I bite my lip and wring my hands together.

'Will ye lassie?' he asks again, a pleading strain in his voice this time. 'No harm in the bandstand.'

'Aye,' I say in a voice barely more than a whisper, 'I will.'

'Willie Lockhart,' he says, his voice as loud as mine is quiet. He thrusts out his hand to shake mine.

'Johanna Blackie,' I whisper and give him my hand.

***

I went to church that Sunday, as I did every Sunday, but couldn't bring myself to look anyone in the eye. That night, after the shame of church I didn't even wait for the bairns to fall asleep. And Willie didn't take himself off to the public house, but I didn't care. I took out my paper. 'Drawing a wee picture, eh?' he said, sucking on his pipe. 'Or making up a wee bit poetry, eh?' I didn't even answer him.

1/6 Harewood Drive
Craigmillar
1st June 1935

My dear James

I am so ashamed. After all these years I am not married! He had a wife all this time. And a daughter! I hang my head when I have to step out of doors for the mortification of it all.

But then I think of you. In all these years my heart was and continues to be yours. It is right I was never married for I never in my deepest heart was. A new hope flames in me. I think you are coming home. Perhaps you are there already. Grace says I must put by hope for even if you did come home you would not be in your right mind. I laugh at such a thing and ask myself – my 'husband' – is he in his 'right mind?' All is turned upside down. Perhaps this is my chance to start again.

Willie says we will go to the Registrar in two weeks for that's how long it takes to display the banns. Then, he says, we'll get married proper.

I can't bear to look at him. He says he thought Rubena was dead but I know that is not true. The police believe him but he was ever the charmer. By rights bigamists should go to jail. I am not the only one writing secret letters. Many a letter he with his copper-plate hand he is so boastful of was sent over the water to his daughter. Faith is her name. If I wasn't so ashamed I might laugh. Faith! Faith's father sits by the poor fire sucking on his pipe, thinking I sit here scribbling poetry. He is an old man and so many lies from him I have had to bear.

James, if I came to you, would you take me in? I have five children – no, hardly children now. They would be a help about the place. I am forty one years old, James. Is it too late? And if you have this terrible shell-shock, I would care for you.

I did try and find you. I took the bus to Crieff and from there a small bus to Comrie. I ran to the boat shed and a man met me there. I thought he said you were dead and I was so overcome with grief I turned and ran.

But I hadn't listened well. For later I thought, he wasn't talking of you. He was talking about his son.

You see, I have never given up hope. When I write these letters I picture you alive and well. Baxter said she would try and find you, and deliver the letters. Of course, with Baxter I never know if she's joking, or telling the truth. And I hope she does find you. Though when I told Grace I still held a candle for you she said I am a dreamer.

Grace is a true friend but she doesn't care for the affairs of the heart. You remember our dear friend and fellow servant Sadie? She was only fifteen and pregnant. My shame now is little compared to hers then. She hung herself from a sycamore tree. From that awful day Grace vowed chastity.

Oh, James. Are you there? Can you hear me? Perhaps Baxter will send this to you.

Will you take my hand? I am a free woman and one who loves you. There is so little to lose, and so much to gain.

Send me a sign, my dearest James.

I love you
Johanna xxx

The fortnight dragged and no letter came from James Melville. No knock came at the door. I walked about like a ghost. I hardly spoke. Or not to Willie at any rate. To my poor bairns I tried to raise a smile and act as normal. But the hardest thing to bear; the look of hate in Donald's eyes for his father. Jamesy remained civil but his speech to his father was clipped and to the point. And I could see the way Gordon ran and hid when Willie came home, the wee boy's fists clenched behind the door like he would strike his own father. Jane was sick of his ways, I could see that. More than once he caught her emptying bottles of beer and whisky down the sink. And she could put him in his place too. If it was possible she hated his drinking even more than I did. Watching her screwed up face as she poured the foul stuff down the sink you'd think it was a vat of rotting eggs she was getting rid of.

Only Mina seemed to love him. She'd be the one to take his coat from him and bend down and untie his shoes. She'd be the one to pat him on the shoulder and join in with his Bolshevik songs. 'Play Annie Laurie faither,' said the one adoring off-spring and so he whipped out his violin and she accompanied him – gie'd me her promise true, she sang, while Donald and Gordon couldn't bring themselves to look at him. Don't hate him, I thought, for all his faults he's your father and the head of the household. Honour your father. Don't hate him.

Towards the end of that terrible fortnight Baxter appeared. It wasn't her visiting day. In fact she'd missed her last two visits, sending word with Grace that she wasn't keeping well. Well, here she was, standing on the doorstep and wringing her old hands together. 'Oh, Blackie,' she said, and she hadn't called me that for years. 'I saw the banns.'

'Come in,' I said, ushering her into the living room. The bairns were all at school, except Jane who had started working in an office. Willie was out, for a walk. That's what I told Baxter, my voice dripping with sarcasm.

She sunk into the armchair by the fire. Poor thing looked exhausted and seeing her sitting there, old, worn and in her cheap brown coat, I stopped feeling pity for myself. 'A cup of tea, Mrs Baxter?' I had kept up the Mrs, even though she was never married. And after she left the Wakeford's she ceased being a cook. But still, she was Mrs Baxter, as I was Miss Blackie.

She nodded, still wringing her hands. While I waited for the kettle to come to the boil I tried to cheer her up. 'Do you think a chicken is good to eat when it's three weeks old?'

She looked up at me, startled. 'No hen, I don't think so.'

'Then how is it going to live?' She didn't laugh. 'It's a joke, Baxter. Do you get it?'

'No, hen,' she said, 'I can't think of anything except you being cheated on all these years. Wit a mannie. You're way too good for him, Blackie.' It was only when I set her tea cup down I saw she had a string bag slung over her arm. She rummaged in it and brought out all the letters I had written to James Melville. 'I cannae tell a lie, Johanna, but I read them and if ye want a bit o advice from an old woman, leave Willie to stew in his own undoing and lies and cheating. There's good love in you, Johanna, and you'll find a man worthy o you. Who knows, but with God's help you might find Mr Melville himself. Or if not him, somebody like him.' She thrust the letters into my shaking hands. 'They make heart-wrenching reading. I'm sorry, Johanna, but when I saw the banns I just had to.'

I scooped them up in my arms, some of them twenty one years old. The paper in some had faded yellow. I felt my own tender heart burst inside me as I clutched the letters to my chest. 'Oh, Baxter,' I said, tears pooling in my eyes.

'Aye, hen,' she murmured, 'aye, I know.'

She didn't finish her tea. She said she didn't want to miss her bus. In the hallway I helped her into her old brown coat. 'I get it now,' she said, 'the joke, I get it.'

As I stood at the door and watched her go down the stairs the thought came to me, the joke was me.

The night before we were due to go to the registrars I laid out my dark blue wool coat and my black leather shoes. I polished them and sat them under the bed, waiting.

I'm nineteen.

Lizzie is ailing and I'm to be promoted to first housemaid. An extra eight shillings a year will be added to my pay. Then the Kaiser comes and changes the lives of millions.

Grange House is commandeered then occupied by officers and turned into a training station. Only the cook and the housekeeper are to be kept on. Not even the butler is wanted. It all happens quickly and with a great deal of noise and bustle. Kists are packed. Rooms are cleared. Dishes and ornaments are hastily wrapped in newspaper and stored in tea chests. 'Europe is being broken up,' is what the Balfours tell us, 'so we're off to the new world.' They have business interests in America and take a ship over the ocean.

James Melville has already gone. Leaving Perthshire feels like leaving him and a piece of myself behind. I want to throw rose petals on the river, but there isn't time. I take the train back to Edinburgh. My kist has more in it now; a small silver locket I bought in Comrie in a jewellers shop. And a new blouse I have made and a hat. And several postcards of boats on the river, and a dress pattern for a calf length skirt. And a good bone comb. I cry leaving Grange House. Of course I cry. We all do. The order and rhythm we worked so hard to create and maintain is gone.

The train journey back to Edinburgh is filled, not with kists, but brown kit bags issued by the war office. Soldiers pile into the train, all grinning from ear to ear as though taking part in the world's biggest party.

Flags and hankies and gloves – anything that can be waved is waved. I watch these soldiers kiss the tear-stained faces of weeping sweethearts on the packed platforms. I hear the rousing songs along the carriage and see young lads, too young to join up, cling to their mother's skirts on the platforms, and I see tearful women singing through their tears, all of them singing:

Oh we don't want to lose you,
But we think you ought to go,
For your King and country,
Both need you so.
We shall want you and miss you
But with all our might and main
We shall cheer you, thank you, kiss you
When you come home again.

30

I pulled the belt tight on my old blue coat and smoothed down the curled lapel. Under my coat I wore my Paisley pattern Sunday dress, though didn't imagine there'd be any need for it. This was to be the sort of wedding where the bride doesn't even take off her coat. Willie had sent Jamesy up to the phone box to order a taxi-cab ages ago. Where was it? I glanced into the hallway mirror and patted my hair down over the thin white scar. I didn't like the face that looked back at me. I pinched my cheeks but God knows I needn't have bothered. I was ashamed enough. I could see it written in my eyes – shame. 'Are you ready mither?' Willie called from the front room. I didn't answer him. I couldn't bring myself to speak, to him nor anyone. Ready? I looked in the glass again. I didn't look like a bride. Deep lines cut into my face. How would you find me now, James Melville? 'It'll be here the noo,' Willie shouted, 'then ye have tae be ready. Ye can't make the taxi-cab wait.'

Ready? I have been ready for seventeen years. I was ready, and green as the new cut grass, walking up the aisle in Haddington Church, blushing, on my ain father's arm.

'If any man or woman can say why these two should not be wed, speak now, or forever hold your peace.'

A hush fell. Clara in the front pew coughed. Someone else shifted in their pew. It was as though, for those five seconds, every Lockhart in the church held their cheating peace.

'Then I pronounce you…'

I brushed a tear away and shut my eyes to the cruel glass. 'Man and wife!'

Ha! What a joke!

Then I heard it, the high screech of the taxi cab brakes. All the poor folks of Craigmillar would no doubt be craning their necks for a glimpse of the grand black taxi cab. It only meant two things in this street – a wedding or a funeral.

Nobody had died. So they'd know. Maybe they knew all along. All these stares and whispers I endured. Good God, was I the only ignorant one around here?

The front door creaked open. I swung round to see my eldest daughter standing on the front doorstep with her hands behind her back. I glanced at her. Bonny she was and a woman herself. I could hardly meet her eyes I was that shamed. 'Here's a wee flower for ye, mother,' she said, bringing a hand out from behind her back. The bright yellow daffodil in her hand looked like the only innocent thing in the world. I shook my head. What did I want with a flower? Faither appeared then in the hall. He took his bowler hat from the stand and put it on, over his old white head. He snatched up the daffodil from Jane's hand and stuck it in his lapel. I heard myself snort. The children huddled by the kitchen door; Jane, Mina, Jamesy, Donald and Gordon. I glanced at them, read their sad eyes, the way their mouths were shut tight. The way Mina bit her lip.

I cleared my throat, sorted my hat and strode out. I could hear Mina weeping in the hallway but didn't heed her. I could walk faster than Willie. I practically ran down the stairs then hurried out towards the taxi-cab. And right enough, half the street were at their net curtains, not even pretending not to gape. I could do nothing but hurry and keep my head bowed. I heard Willie panting to keep up with me and the words of an old song taunted me – *never marry an auld man*. He was old the first time I married him. He was seventeen years older now, and so was I. An old woman myself.

I only looked up when the taxi, with us inside it, turned around in the street, its brakes screeching. And there they were, at least twenty neighbours, all gawking at the shiny black taxi. I could imagine the silence between them shattering into gossip as soon as the taxi bore Willie and me off to be wed.

Did ye see that scowl on her face?

The puir soul.

Aye, her that hangs oot such a lovely washing tae.

Where d'ye think they're aff tae?

Oh aye, him all sober for once and her dressed up like that.

Getting married – again – that's where!

No?

Away!

I'm telling ye!

Jings, crivens, help ma Boab – really?

Aye really. The whole pub kens.

Him? The old drunkard? Married taw sumbudy else a' this time?

Shame on it.

And wi' a lassie in America.

She'll no be holding her head quite so high in church noo, that's for sure.

Wit a scandal. Her no even proper married. Living in sin a' they years. And a' they bairns. Bastards every one o' them.

These thoughts jabbed and jeered at me, bringing me as low as I ever felt in my life. As though that wasn't bad enough riding in the taxi gave me a sore head with the fumes belching out from the engine and the way we were jigged up and down. It made my stomach churn. And it wasn't only the people from Craigmillar who stared. It seemed everyone in Edinburgh gaped as the taxi slowly bumped its way over the uneven cobbled stones to the registrar's office.

'We'll need a couple o witnesses mother,' Willie said.

'We've got the whole street,' I blurted out. My silence snapped.

'Wheesht mother,' Willie said, nodding towards the cab driver.

'Don't tell me to wheesht.' We rode the rest of the way in silence.

The taxi cab dropped us off outside the registry office and I stood at the door of the place, staring down at my black shoes, while Willie went only a few yards. I glanced up to see him nod to two men, slip them a coin then in we all trouped.

'It's a wee job for them,' he whispered to me, nodding towards the shabbily dressed witnesses, and then we were in the cheerless building. No organ music. No flowers. I thought of Jane's wee daffodil. I saw it droop in Willie's lapel. I imagined a field of daffodils in the spring time, around Grange house. It was that I saw as I walked up that dark brown carpet, and it was Miss Macdonald's soft voice I heard, accompanying me up the aisle; *I wandered lonely as a cloud, that floats on high o'er vale and hill...*

'Mr William Lockhart and Miss Johanna Blackie?' a man's voice called out. Willie waved to the man. I couldn't even look up. The brown carpet had a stain on it. It looked as if oil had spilled. Now Borax would have lifted that if they'd caught it and seen to it early enough. It's no good leaving stains. Then you're with them for ever.

The brown carpet dissolved and turned into a river and the walls of the registry office fell away.

And I am stepping into the rowing boat and the handsome oarsman is taking my hand. It's a strong hand, a hand I can trust. A hand that will catch me if I fall. But I don't fall. The boat wobbles and I laugh. 'There you go, Johanna,' he says and then he sits down beside me and we travel down the river, the music of the hymns still bright in my mind. Abide with me, we both sing.

The registrar coughed. I glanced up at him, surprised to see him. He had a thick black moustache and he turned towards Willie. 'Will you, William Lockhart,' he said, 'take Johanna Blackie to be your lawfully wedded wife?'

'I do.'

There was a swirling in my head. I thought I might fall.

The voice of James Melville, whispering in my ear, 'marry me, Johanna?'

I press my fingers tight around his, and can hardly get the words out for the joy in me. 'Yes, yes, I'll marry you.'

'And do you, Johanna Blackie, take this man, William Lockhart, to be your lawfully wedded husband?' Now the man with the handlebar moustache was staring at me. But the swirling in my head got worse.

'As soon as it's over I'll be straight back. By Christmas, that's what they're saying. Then God help me, I'll marry you,' he says, running his strong fingers through my hair. He kisses me and the boat drifts and my heart bursts with love. I am happy. I am in a field of poppies. I am dreaming.

Willie nudged me. 'Mither,' he hissed. 'It's your turn.'

He was right for once; it was my turn. I stared down. The stain was like a ring on the carpet. Like a cup stain. Like a blood stain on a sheet. I fancied I could hear the skipping rope whirring through the air and all the bairns of Leith crying –

House to let
Apply within
A woman put out
For drinking gin.

I heard the witnesses shuffle in their shoes. Willie was coughing. He nudged me again. The man with the thick moustache standing at the desk in front of us looked anxiously from me to Willie and back to me again. He spoke louder, in case I was deaf. 'I repeat – do you, Johanna Blackie, take this man, William Lockhart, to be your lawful wedded husband?'

A shiver ran up the back of my neck. They were all staring at me now. My head was still in a swirl. And I thought, maybe he didn't die after all? The man in the boat shed was talking about his son. Perhaps James Melville was alive. Willie thought Rubena was dead. That's what Willie was whispering to me now, 'mither, I thought she wis dead,' but I didn't care about Rubena. Or Faith. What a name. Faith.

I lifted my head and looked straight at the man with the moustache. He lifted his bushy eyebrows. 'No,' I whispered.

The registrar twitched his moustache. 'Speak up, Miss Blackie,' he said, leaning towards me.

So I said it again, louder this time. 'No.'

The registrar looked pleadingly at Willie. Help! His pale eyes were crying. Help! The witnesses coughed and patted their chests. I could hear everything so clearly. I could see everything so clearly. The stain on the carpet. The dust motes swirling in the air. The scuff on my good shoes. The veins standing out on the back of my hand. The smell of linseed oil and musty paper. The chip on the white plate that for some reason sat on the desk in front of me.

James Melville was not dead. The man at the boatshed was meaning his own son. I couldn't breathe properly. I pictured the green hills bathed in golden sunlight. I'll walk to the hills, I was thinking. I'll get proper boots and a compass, and I'll go. 'A cup of tea,' someone was saying. It was the man at the desk. He waved to someone at the back of the room. 'We will postpone the ceremony for ten minutes. Make Miss Blackie a cup of tea. Sweet tea. She is just overcome.' The registrar's big face loomed down on me. He had red veins in his nose, like Willie. 'Miss Blackie,' he said, slowly, loudly. 'My secretary here is making you a cup of tea.' He thought I was stupid – daft-straw heid. A lunatic from the asylum. 'There's a wee room just off to the side here.' He was shouting, as if I am a deaf lunatic. 'It's quiet in there. I suggest you sit down. In there,' he said. 'And drink your tea. Gather your thoughts, Miss Blackie.' He carved each word in the air. Willies slumped down on a chair and the witnesses were looking around, like they are at a museum. Willie glared up at me. 'Mother,' he said, 'don't shame me.'

'Shame ye?' I held his gaze till he looked away. I wanted to shout it out. Shame ye? Shame ye? But they took me away for a cup of tea. A woman in a dark red hat took me by the elbow. I looked down and saw her slim hand pressed down over my blue sleeve. I hadn't even taken my coat off, even though I had my best blouse on underneath, all pressed. I could smell Willie's pipe smoke. At my back I heard someone explaining to the witnesses that they were taking a short break. Just ten minutes, they said, then we'll start again. I heard the witnesses asking Willie for more money. I was led into the little room and settled into a chair, as if I was an invalid. Then she handed me the tea, in a fine china cup. 'Do you want me to stir it for you?' the woman in the red hat said.

31

Mother takes me and Jemima up to Princes Street Gardens the day they open the new Floral Clock.

Everybody's cheering and waving their hankies when the cuckoo comes out to announce the hour, and the clock face is a hundred bright flowers. What a fine day that is. And mother enjoys it. She stops frowning and seems pleased to be up the town with her two youngest daughters and us all in our best hats and well-polished boots. We dander about for ages through the lovely gardens and gaze up at the castle on the rock till she says our necks are going to break, then when the one o'clock gun goes off we all jump out of our skins.

Mother doesn't cook dinner that day. We get fish and chips from a shop and eat them in newspaper while we sit on a bench in Princes Street gardens. My, how we rabbit on, like three happy bairns, about the flowers and all the colours and the scents and best of all – the cuckoo. Oh, the cuckoo!

'Did you see how it came out all by itself?'

'Aye, just on the hour. I swear it sounds just like a real one.'

'I've never heard a real cuckoo.'

'And the bonny flowers. Did you ever see so many colours? You could make a posy for a bride.'

And we giggle then, me and Jemima.

***

The tea was strong. The woman heaped sugars into it. 'There is another wedding after your one, Miss Blackie,' said the secretary, but she smiled at me and I smiled back. 'So we can only give you ten minutes to gather your thoughts.' I was thinking about the cloche hat on her head. And how daring to wear red. She turned and walked towards the door, leaving me sitting in the wee room to the side of the main registry room. It was like a cloakroom. I could see coats on the coat stand. And a bowler hat. There were no windows in the wee room. For a second I thought of Mr Mahoney, and wondered where he was now. The woman stopped at the door and looked back at me, her hand resting on the door handle. 'Miss Blackie?' she said.

I lifted my head and looked at her.

'You don't have to, you know.'

I sipped the tea, staring at her over the rim of the cup. 'I know.'

I am lying in my little bed in the attic.

I am so filled up with boats and rivers and hands and coconut shies and tea and sandwiches and raspberries and cream and sunshine and cherry blossom and fires and squibs and Catherine wheels I don't want to leave it to slip into the nothingness of sleep. My stump of candle trickles wax onto the stool by my bed. The moon shines through the small window, falling on my cheeks. I feel the strong and gentle fingers of the oarsman as he strokes my cheek. I think how the moon and all its dreams will be falling on the young blushing faces of all the young servant girls who sleep in attic rooms, all dreaming of this Victoria holiday; girls with kists at the ends of their beds, girls dreaming of marriage and white horses, pearl necklaces and bonny bairns, who will rise at dawn to set fires in cold rooms, shoo mice from the drawing rooms of the gentry and cast their eyes down when the mistress shuffles past in her dressing gown, farting with every step, girls who are seen and not heard, who gather up their thick hair into mutch caps and bind their breasts with strips of cloth. Girls who stem their monthly flow with a thick wad of cloth which they boil over and over. Girls with hands that work fourteen hours a day, with a script deep in their palms that says it will always be so. Girls whose mothers have done the same – and their mothers before them. Girls who learn to say yes.

'They'll be getting a' they modern gadgets to replace us,' says Baxter. The three of us are sitting round the servant's fire, toil weary the lot of us. 'Just you mark my words.' Her trusty sense of humour seems to have failed her.

'No gadget will ever work as hard as yourself, Mrs Baxter,' says Grace, who has taken her boots off and is sitting with her feet up on a stool.

'Don't you believe it. Ha! This war's spoiling everything. Everything! Fine folks don't entertain like they used to, so we're not needed like we used to be. I overheard Mrs Wakeford say that to the maister just the other day. She said with a few o' they modern contraptions they could cut back on servants. Goodness mercy me – there's just the three o' us. Who would they cut back on? Me!'

'Never,' I say, patting Baxter on the arm. She's getting beside herself, twisting her red chapped hands like she is trying to prize a ring from swollen fingers. 'Never,' I repeat, stronger this time, 'the Wakefords are good Christians. They'll never let you go.'

'Oh aye they would. I heard them Miss Blackie, on about the taxes and the price o' food and everything. They're no as rich as they used to be. Aye, it's me they'll send to the poorhouse. Auld Baxter. Thrown out like an old pit pony.'

'Don't be talking like that Mrs Baxter. You are a faithful servant – and a good cook.'

'Well – who needs a cook when you get a contraption to do it for you? Electric servants, that's what they'll have next. No, you two are the young ones. I'm auld. Done for!'

There's no comforting her. And anyway, maybe she's right.

***

The loudest thing in the little room was the clock. What a din with the ticking. I wrapped my hands about the tea cup. The tea was going cold. The ticking was going on. It was nearly two o'clock. I was forty two. And the ticking is louder.

Then I am thirty two, twenty two. I am teetering on the edge of the chair. My thoughts spin. My hands are shaking. I am nineteen. I am afraid the fine bone china cup will fall.

The candle flame flickers out as I slip into the sweet darkness of sleep and all that night, I swear, Mr James Melville rows me down a never ending river. And I dream and in that dream I say yes. And I reach out and take his hand.

There was a little hill of sugar at the bottom of the cup.

I'm writing my letter to the agency.

I form my letters well and tell them how I'm free from disease, a hard worker, a Christian and extremely interested in the post of second housemaid in the house in Perthshire. My fingers are trembling. I seal the envelope and hide the letter under my bed. I can't sleep. My stomach's churning with images of grand stone houses where every bay window is hung with velvet drapes and happy servants flit noiselessly to and fro, happy making order, and nobody falls down drunk.

I keep the letter secret. Mother will find out soon enough and well I know what father thinks of picking up fallen napkins for the upper classes.

***

I scoop some of the wet sugar out with the wee spoon they gave me. The clock kept ticking, louder and louder. I could see Willie's face in the round face of the clock. Willie Lockhart, the watchmaker, a fine thing to be. Suddenly I was filled with panic. The woman with the red hat would come and open the door any moment now. I held tight to the cup and saucer. I had been dreaming, my head swirling. Now in a panic I remembered exactly where I was, and why. I remembered who I was. Johanna Blackie. I remembered my responsibilities. The shame. The children. The bastards. You've made your bed, now lie in it. Yes, I said out loud. No, I said. Yes. No. Yes. No. You don't have to, you know. I do. I do not. The seconds hammer on.

On Princes Street there are grand shops to look at.

You can hardly tell there's a war on. The shops are full of fine displays, not like in some of the wee shops in Leith. Some of them have to close down for lack of stuff to sell. In the confectioner's window at the foot of The Walk all you see are big empty glass jars with not a sweetie in sight. I sigh and remember a red gobstopper and a kiss from Geordie McPhee. Where is he now? Dead?

But up on Princes Street there are sweets to be had if you have the money to come by them. And if you have money you can find mourning clothes, rich red carpets from the east, Belfast sinks, wash basins and rose-patterned jugs, petticoats and wide-brimmed hats, linen blouses and silver buttons, tweed blankets, silk stockings and ball gowns.

'If – just imagine if,' says Sadie, 'you were invited to a ball – which dress would you go in?' We all stare at the glorious ball gowns in the window as if some fairy godmother might suddenly appear and wave a magic wand.

'That one,' I say after a serious scrutiny of them all. I point to a long dove grey satin dress with a scooped neck line – just like the dress my mother said Mary Pickford wore in her last film.

'Yes Johanna,' says Grace, nodding thoughtfully, 'that would go very well with your black hair. But you'll need a necklace to set off the neckline. Aye, your dress definitely needs a necklace.' I agree with her and so us servant girls on our half day off set off along the street to stare in the jeweller's window.

We spend hours doing that. None of us will ever go to a ball and well we know it. But all of us can dream.

I check the clock. It seems I have been here my whole life. I can't believe only five minutes have passed. But the tea is tepid. Perhaps they have forgotten me? Sadie is dead. Perhaps there are grand balls in heaven? I twist a button on my coat. Perhaps Willie has gone off to the public house with the witnesses? Grace would help me and the bairns, until we are on our feet. Grace would help us out. She said she would. She never did approve of Willie Lockhart. He wasn't even in the war. Not the proper war. And she can't abide lies.

They say we're winning the war. Even though the fields of France are filled with Scottish blood the newsreels tell us in their fast crackling voices that it will soon be over. Grace and I have taken to sitting by the fire after the days' work and in low tones we talk about the awful war and how we'll be spinsters and aren't we lucky we can work to keep ourselves? Baxter is already a resigned spinster and is forever saying how young Grace and I are. I don't feel young. I am twenty four, almost twenty five – and not a prospective husband in sight.

'Can't say I'm sorry Johanna.' It was after what happened to Sadie. Grace swore then she'd never marry.

'But what about bairns? Don't you want some Grace?'

'There are plenty bairns in the world. If you have bairns, Johanna, I'll dandle them on my knee.'

'Me too,' says Baxter, suddenly brightening up at the thought of bairns. 'Have lots, Johanna. That'll give me something to knit for.'

I stare at Grace and Baxter. 'But James,' I say, his name turning my voice to a whisper, 'is gone.'

Grace and Baxter look at each other. 'Well, he might be,' Baxter says, 'or he might turn up yet.' But her voice lacks conviction.

'And anyway,' Grace says, 'there's a few more fish in the sea.'

***

I sipped the cold tea. I scooped up the last of the sugar. I glanced at the clock.

James Melville didn't die. I felt certain of that now.

Time was running on. And I remembered how I told wee Jane, I'll have to go back and take all the bairns God gives me.

In our small attic bedroom the rain mists the window panes.

Its sound gives a quiet pattering to the night. I pull off my mutch cap, shake my head and let my hair fall down. 'I know nothing about men, nothing at all,' I say, my voice low and halting in the dark. 'I'm scared Grace. It doesn't feel right. I don't want to … '

'Then don't,' she whispers, already tucked up in bed.

I climb into my narrow bed and pull the blanket up to my chin. Grace doesn't know. She doesn't know what it's like. She'll never marry. 'But, I have to,' I whisper.

'Then do what you have to.'

And to that I can only whisper goodnight, my last day's work as a servant done.

'Good-night to you too, Johanna,' she whispers. A tear streams down my cheek.

***

I could see a dark shadow at the glass of the door. I could see the curved shape of her cloche hat. It was the woman who brought me the tea. I glanced at the clock. Hickory-dickory dock. Ten minutes exactly.

James Melville is rowing his boat on the river and I am standing on the bank waving. I do want to marry a good woman.

The woman in the hat didn't even bother to knock. She was opening the door. I could see the brass knob turning.

The way Willie kicked the door open, me just wed and scooped in his arms, and the way my young heart sank at the pokiness of the place. I see James Melville's strong hand reaching to take my gloved hand and help me into the boat. My hand is trembling. The boat wobbles on the water. He is alive. I will go to him. I will give him my hand.

The woman in the red hat stepped in to the little room. 'Now then,' she said. I gasped. The cup shook in my hand. I tried to place it on the saucer. It slipped. The cup dropped from my hand. It fell to the ground and shattered. Pieces of china spilled out. I could see how the broken pieces caught the lamplight as they fell. The woman stood in the middle of the room. We both stared down at the broken cup, and at the pattern it made on the floor. Then the woman took a step towards me.

'Johanna Blackie,' she said, 'it's time.'